Victor Doublet

Logic for young ladies

Translated from the French

Victor Doublet

Logic for young ladies
Translated from the French
ISBN/EAN: 9783741185328

Manufactured in Europe, USA, Canada, Australia, Japa

Cover: Foto ©Andreas Hilbeck / pixelio.de

Manufactured and distributed by brebook publishing software
(www.brebook.com)

Victor Doublet

Logic for young ladies

LOGIC

FOR YOUNG LADIES,

TRANSLATED FROM THE FRENCH

OF

VICTOR DOUBLET,

PROFESSOR OF BELLES-LETTRES.

LOGIC TEACHES HOW TO REASON, TO JUDGE, TO DISCOVER TRUTH, AND
TO MAKE IT KNOWN TO OTHERS; IT IS, AS IT WERE,
THE KEY TO ALL THE OTHER SCIENCES.

NEW YORK:

P. O'SHEA, PUBLISHER,

27 BARCLAY STREET.

TABLE OF SUBJECTS.

FIRST PART,
Of Perception or Ideas.

CHAPTER I.

ARTICLE 1.

ARTICLE 2.

CHAPTER II.

SECOND PART,
Of Judgment.

CHAPTER I.

THIRD PART,

Of Reasoning.

CHAPTER I.

CHAPTER II.

ARTICLE 1.

ARTICLE 2.

FOURTH PART.
Of Method.

INTRODUCTION.

UTILITY OF LOGIC.

To ask whether Logic is useful, is to ask whether the study of all the sciences is advantageous. At the present day especially, when people generally admit the necessity of acquiring knowledge, at a period when information is spread abroad and propagated rapidly through every class of society, it would be loss of time to undertake to prove the utility of studying the various sciences, among which Logic may be considered the principal, I may even say the most important.

In truth, Logic is, as it were, the key of all other sciences; it opens to us the door of Truth in every department of learning, thus enabling us to avoid the paths of error.

Men, having perceived that they happened frequently to fall into the abyss of error, have sought rules and principles upon which they may form their thoughts, pursue and direct them, in order to attain a knowledge of truth, and avoid the by-paths that lead away from it; and they have given the name Logic, that is, the art

1*

of reasoning, to the system which collects these
principles, observations, and maxims, the knowl- •
edge of which may give the human mind more
penetration, power, extension, accuracy and facility, whether in the pursuit of truth, or in
comprehending it when proposed by others, or
in fine when communicating it after it is acquired.

Hitherto this science (whose utility is so generally admitted) has been sealed in learned
tomes, thus depriving young ladies of facility in
learning it, at least until they entered the highest classes; and as many do not complete the
full course of studies at present exacted in acade-
mies, this branch has been left unacquired. This
should not be. Women have as much need of
reasoning as the sterner sex. They are daily
called upon to direct affairs of great importance,
and sometimes even to hold the reins of government.

It is precisely because women are deemed
prone to inconsiderateness that they should be
early accustomed to reflect, to render an account
of their thoughts, and to draw just conclusions;
they will then be found later, capable of sowing
the seeds of early instruction and of sound logic
in the minds of those whom their position obliges
them to instruct.

Let young ladies beware of being repelled by
the difficulties and dryness which they discover
in the pursuit of this study; the highest and the
most abstract sciences have been grasped by the

gentler sex, and many ladies have attained celebrity in the pursuit of profound learning.

The translator would merely add that she has found that the text-books on Logic, hitherto offered to American teachers, contain doctrines and illustrations which it is unnecessary to present to pupils, at least until they enter the higher classes. She has, therefore, aimed at supplying a want felt by judicious and conscientious instructors of young ladies, to whom she humbly dedicates her little work of zeal.

LOGIC FOR YOUNG LADIES.

DEFINITION OF THE SCIENCE.

Question. What is Logic?

Answer. Logic is a science which teaches how *to think, to reason, to judge, to discover truth* and *communicate it to others;* it is, as it were, *the key* to all the other sciences.

It may also be defined a Practical Science, which serves to direct the thoughts of the mind.

Q. Explain this definition?

A. 1st. I call it *Science*, because it appropriately pertains to science to demonstrate by certain arguments the precision of the rules it lays down. Logic fulfils perfectly this condition, for it teaches that a definition should be clearer than the thing defined, and should also explain its nature; in addition to which it sustains its rules by syllogisms and sure principles.

2d. I call it *Practical Science*, because it prescribes certain rules, by means of which we may attain to the knowledge of the various subjects of which it treats.

3d. It directs the faculties of the mind; these are perception, judgment, reasoning, and method. The object of Logic is to improve these faculties, to rectify the judgment, and classify ideas.

These four faculties of the mind form the four divisions of Logic, and will become subjects of four dissertations; but as it will be necessary to argue from the very beginning of this study, we will, before proceeding further, give a general view of argumentation. The art of reasoning, or of argumentation, will be more fully developed in the dissertation that will be given hereafter.

OF ARGUMENTATION, OR REASONING.

Thought, or ideas, judgment, and reasoning, are the cause, or the origin, of all the actions of men, the source of good and evil; for the idea, or thought, is either good or bad; the judgment shows it clearly, and the judgment determines the will.

Before entering upon the subject, we will define these three faculties which seem to keep our intellect in a state of continual activity.

Q. What is an idea?

A. It is the reflection of an object in the mind. If an object is held before a mirror, the mirror will faithfully reflect all the features and an exact outline of the object thus presented; so the mind reflects the objects that are presented to it, interiorly or exteriorly.

Example.—If I think of God, purely and simply, without adding any thing to the idea of God, that is, not thinking of His attributes, this is a simple thought, or rather an idea.

Q. What is judgment?

A. It is an act of the mind, by which two ideas are compared, with a view of examining their agreement or their disagreement. There are two kinds of judgment—the affirmative judgment, by which we affirm that a certain quality is applicable to a being, or object; and the negative judgment, by which we deny a certain quality to a certain being, or object.

Q. Give an example of an affirmative judgment?

A. God is just.

Q. How do you prove that this judgment is affirmative?

A. By saying "God is just," I have affirmed that the quality of justice is applicable to God.

Q. Give an example of a negative judgment.

A. God is not cruel.

Q. How do you prove that this judgment is negative?

A. In saying God is not cruel I remove from the idea of God the idea of *cruelty* which succeeded my first idea, because I deemed it incompatible with the first idea.

Q. Explain further the difference that exists between idea and judgment.

A. An idea is merely the reflection of an object in our mind; judgment, on the contrary, is the comparison, union, or disjunction of two ideas with or from one another. From the idea springs the judgment, from the judgment springs the proposition.

Q. What is a proposition?

A. It is the enunciation or expression of a judgment.

Example.—If I have formed an idea in thinking of God, I shall form a judgment in thinking that God is good; and if I do not content myself with merely thinking so, but express these two ideas by saying to a person: God is good—I have formed a proposition.

Examples.—Snow is white. Water is fluid. Vice is not commendable.

Q. How many parts does a proposition include?

A. A proposition includes three parts, which

are: The subject, the verb (called also the copula), and the predicate.

Q. What is the subject?

A. It is that concerning which a judgment, either affirmative or negative is declared.

Q. What is the verb, or copula?

A. It is the bond which unites the predicate to the subject; it is always expressed by the verb *to be*.

Example.—Religion *is* indispensable to happiness. Here the word *is* forms the copula, joining *religion*, the subject, with indispensable to happiness, the predicate.

Q. What is reasoning?

A. It is a mental operation by which we deduce a judgment (or conclusion) from one or several other judgments. If, for instance, I say, "Every virtue is pleasing to God;" now, modesty is a virtue, therefore, modesty is pleasing to God; the act by which I deduce my conclusion from the two preceding judgments is called reasoning.

Q. How many parts does reasoning include?

A. Reasoning includes three parts, which are, the antecedent, the consequent, and the consequence.

Q. What is the antecedent?

A. The antecedent is the first part of reasoning; from it the two others are derived; it is generally formed of an axiom. It is also called the premises.

Q. What is an axiom?

A. It is a certain, or self-evident proposition, that no one can doubt; as two and two make four; the circle is round; God exists.

Q. What is the consequent?

A. It is the second term of any relation; it is that second part of reasoning which is naturally deduced from the preceding term; it is also called a conclusion.

Q. What is a consequence?

A. It is the result of the reasoning, or rather it is the union of the conclusion with the premises. This union in the mind is an act by which, from the truth of two judgments, the mind deduces the truth of a third.

Q. Give an instance of reasoning which contains these three parts very distinctly.

A. Every vice is contemptible.

Ant.—Sloth is a vice.

Con.—Hence, sloth is contemptible.

The first two propositions are called the antecedent, or the premises; the last is called the conclusion, or the consequent; it follows from the two others. The union of the conclusion

with the antecedent, or the premises, is called
the consequence.

Q. What is argumentation?

A. It is reasoning, expressed in language.

Q. How many kinds of argumentation are
there?

A. Two principal ones, viz.: syllogism and
enthymeme.

Q. What is a syllogism?

A. It is an argument formed of three propositions, so blended and so necessary to each other
that the third follows naturally from the two
preceding, as in this example:—

Every virtue is laudable.

Temperance is a virtue.

Therefore, temperance is laudable.

Q. How many terms does the syllogism contain?

A. It is composed of three terms, which are:
The great extreme, or *major;* the less extreme,
or *minor;* and the *middle term,* or conclusion,
which is the idea with which we compare the
two others.

Q. Apply these rules to the syllogism just presented.

A. *Laudable* is the major, *temperance* the minor, and *virtue* the middle term. The minor
term is the subject of the conclusion, and the

major term is its predicate. It is called major, because it has usually more extension than the subject, or the minor term. The predicate *laudable* is far more extensive than *temperance*, because there are a great number of things different from temperance which are, nevertheless, laudable. We compare, in one of the premises, the *major* term, *laudable*, with the middle term, *virtue*, and we see clearly that the idea of virtue is contained in the idea of laudable. In the second of the premises, we compare the minor term, *temperance*, with the middle term, *virtue*, and we perceive that it is included in that middle term.

Q. Thence, what do you conclude?

A. That the *minor* is included in the *major*, or that the *major* and *minor* agree with each other.

Q. How many propositions does a syllogism contain?

A. A syllogism contains three propositions, which are commonly called the major, the minor, and the conclusion.

Q. What is the major?

A. It is that which contains the *great extreme* with the middle term, as in the above syllogism: Every virtue is laudable.

Q. What is the minor?

A. The minor is that proposition which in-

cludes the *less extreme* with the *middle term.*
As in the same example: Temperance is a virtue. The major and the minor together are
called the premises, because they always precede
the conclusion.

Q. What is the conclusion?

A. It is that proposition of the syllogism
which contains the great extreme, as in this:
Therefore, temperance is laudable.

Q. What is an enthymeme?

A. It is an argument which contains only two
propositions, one of which is deduced from the
other, and the first of which is called the ante
cedent and the second the consequent.

All good is amiable.

Therefore, God is amiable.

We perceive that this kind of reasoning differs
from the syllogism in that one of the premises
is commonly understood; sometimes it is the
major, sometimes it is the minor, that is understood.

Justice is a virtue.

Therefore justice is praiseworthy.

In the first example, we have understood the
minor, God is the supreme good; and in the
second we have left the major understood:
Every virtue is praiseworthy. The proposition
expressed is easily understood in each of these

two examples ; whence it is said that the enthymeme expressed is a real syllogism in thought.

Q. What are the rules of syllogisms ?

A. There are two principal ones, which are called general rules ; one regards affirmative syllogisms and the other negative syllogisms.*

RULE FOR AFFIRMATIVE SYLLOGISMS.

When the premises are affirmative, the conclusion must also be affirmative. In truth, if two proposed ideas are compared with a third, and it be found that they both agree with that third, it is certain that all three of the terms agree. The character of *Creator* agrees with *God*, and *worship* agrees with a Creator ; therefore *worship* agrees with *God*.

Q. Give us an example that will aid us to understand this clearly.

A. If I compare Mary with Josephine, and I find that both are of the same height, and then comparing Clara and Josephine, I find that they also are of the same height, it is evident that Mary and Clara are equally tall ; hence, when two objects correspond equally to a third, they are equal to each other.

Thus, if the major is affirmative, it declares

* For all the other rules of syllogisms we refer to the dissertation on Reasoning.—3d Part, Art. I.

that the *greater extreme* agrees with the *middle term*. So, when the minor is affirmative, it shows that the *less extreme* agrees with the middle term. Now, the two extremes can not agree with the same middle term, without agreeing with each other; and this suitability can not be otherwise expressed than by an affirmative conclusion; hence, when the premises are affirmative, the conclusion must also be affirmative.

Hence, when two objects, taken singly, are equal to a third, they are equal to each other.

RULES FOR NEGATIVE SYLLOGISMS.

When one of the premises is affirmative and the other negative, the conclusion must be negative.

For, when *one* of the premises is negative and the other affirmative, it happens that of the two extremes one agrees with the middle term, and the other does not agree with it. Thence, it follows that the two extremes differ from each other; now, this difference can only be expressed by a negative conclusion; therefore, when *one* of the premises is affirmative and the other negative, the conclusion must be negative.

Q. What axiom serves as a basis for this rule?

A. When one of two propositions agrees with a third, and the other does not agree with it, these two propositions do not agree with each other. Or rather, when of two objects, one is equal to a third, and the other is not equal to it, these two objects differ from each other.

Q. Explain this to us more clearly by an example.

A. If Mary is as tall as Josephine, and Clara is not as tall as Josephine, it is clear that Clara and Mary are not of equal height.

Q. Are philosophical discussions useful?

A. Yes, for they are very well calculated to exercise the mind and rectify the judgment; they cause young persons to contract a habit of answering with propriety, accuracy, and clearness; they render the mind more ready and more intelligent.

But we must beware of falling into the defect so common among logicians, who, by dint of subtleties, raise questions which it is impossible for them to solve; and the consequences that they accumulate, disturb and at length overthrow the principles which they had at first laid down. They wander, only to find themselves obliged to return.

Thus Montaigne said, when speaking of false logic: "It does not render men wiser or more capable; those who are governed by it do not live better or think more justly."

But this censure can not be applied to sound logic, whose rules teach us to follow with greater facility and success those paths that conduct to Truth. They also aid us to reject errors into which we have fallen, or to which we may be in danger of adhering, either through dullness of intellect, tenacity, or the effects of a faulty education.

To conclude, the principles of sound logic justly merit our serious attention, as they treat of the nobler part of our nature. They inform us in what order our thoughts arise, succeed each other, expand and improve; they show us what relation exists between them and the terms by which they are expressed; they distinguish their various species and disclose their properties; they reveal to us the cause of our mistakes, and show us how to anticipate and avoid them in future. These are, therefore, the inestimable advantages offered to you, of which you should eagerly hasten to profit.

FIRST PART.

Perception may be defined an act by which the soul knows or perceives what passes within or without it. In the first case it is called interior perception; in the second, exterior perception.

CHAPTER I.

OF INTERIOR PERCEPTION.

Question. What is an Idea or Perception?

Answer. Idea or perception, considered in respect to its existence in the mind itself, may also be considered either in respect to itself, or in reference to its action on the mind.

Illus.: The idea is in the mind itself, and can Have no existence but in a mind that thinks; but the remote or mediate object may be something external as the sun or moon; it may be something past or future; it may be something that never existed.

Example of an idea: An architect who is em-

2

ployed to erect a new structure forms at first in his mind an idea of that building, but he gives it expression when he executes the work.

ARTICLE FIRST.

OF IDEA, OR PERCEPTION CONSIDERED IN ITSELF.

Question. Define idea.

Answer. Idea in a philosophical sense, means some image, or representation of an external object present to the mind. And

1st. I say representation, because if you ask me what equality I find between twice two and four, I can only answer that I conceive it distinctly, but I can not prove it to you, because it is one of those truths perceived so easily that we style them axioms; an axiom, we have already observed, is a truth so evident, that to doubt it would be exposing ourselves to be considered either destitute of reason, or devoid of that common sense with which nature endows the greatest number of reasonable creatures.

2d. I call it a simple representation, because I but perceive it, without addition or subtraction, without affirmation or negation.

Q. Can nothing, or an object which does not exist, be perceived or form an idea?

A. No; for we can only perceive a being or an existence; now as nothing is a nonentity, we can not perceive it, neither can we represent it under any form whatever; hence nothing can not form an idea; for according to an axiom generally adopted, nothing has no property.

Q. Can the impossible be considered as possible ?

A. No; because the impossible is a veritable nonentity, and the mind can not conceive an exact idea of naught; for the mind is accustomed to compare objects in order to deduce conclusions concerning them : it considers their defects, their good qualities, and their properties ; now with what other object could the mind compare the impossible so as to derive or form an idea, since the impossible has neither form, nor qualities, nor defects, nor properties, since in a word it does not exist ? The impossible, therefore, can not be considered as possible.

Q. However, are there not some things that we usually consider impossible, and which are, nevertheless, not only possible but real, since they are narrated by historians worthy of credit, and are sometimes supported by the testimony of distinguished personages?

Commor, an English physician, assures us that when he was at the court of the king of

Poland, a man was brought in whom they had taken from a troop of bears with which he ran about, using his arms as a second pair of legs. He was, says he, little less fierce than a bear, could not endure the eyes of other men, and stood up by bracing his hands against the walls: by degrees they tamed him and taught him to talk.

The same author adds that the bears frequently carry away the children of laborers, when they leave their little ones cradled among the leaves, while they are occupied with their daily toil; and he conjectures that a female bear, incommoded by excess of her milk may have acted as nurse to the infant she had borne away.

Procopius relates that during a war in Italy, all the inhabitants of a village having fled at the approach of an enemy, an infant that had been forgotten was suckled by the goats, and that he learned to roam with them through the woods and over the rocks.

How will you explain the possibility of such facts, as they appear to be utterly impossible? Besides, you have declared that the impossible can never be considered possible, for the impossible is a nonentity. In the above facts I prove clearly that the impossible may be considered possible, for it exists; it being impossible that a wild female bear, naturally cruel (perhaps, too, pressed by hunger), would not have eaten a defenseless babe; but yet, the female bear not only did not devour it, but according to this author, she must have actually nourished it with her own milk?

A. There are in nature monsters, or rather wonders that we can not conceive, because they surpass the weakness of our understanding; but because we do not comprehend an extraordinary thing which is above our intelligence, and because we can not account for it, must we therefore conclude that it is impossible?

It also appears to be an impossibility that a child could learn to run about with goats, and follow them through woods and over mountains; but these are extraordinary things, or phenomena, like those fantastic shapes that nature occasionally takes pleasure in displaying to mankind; there is in these recitals nothing that is impossible, at most they are but marvelous; hence they can never suffice to prove that the impossible may be considered possible.

Q. But in dreams, do we not sometimes see impossible things, and things which have no existence traced in our imagination, under certain and determinate forms? The impossible and naught or ponentity may therefore be considered possible, and even visible under certain forms or appearances.

A. Dreams can only be considered as wander·
ings of the imagination, which during sleep is not
controlled by the judgment or will; besides, memory is also without guide, and can not direct
the imagination or retrace the objects which
have been confided to it (or rather which have
been hastily presented to it); it is therefore incapable of rendering an exact account of these
same ideas. Now, we can never assume for re-
alities the errors of an imagination that is
continually wandering from the point; hence
dreams do not prove that the impossible may be
considered possible; therefore nothing, or a nonentity, can not be presented to the mind in any
real form.

ARTICLE SECOND.

OF IDEAS CONSIDERED IN THEIR ACTION ON THE MIND.

The first and most fruitful of the operations
of the mind, is reflection. From it are derived
as from their natural source, the combining of
ideas, abstraction and precision, comparison, distinction, and distribution.

Question. What is reflection?

Answer. It is an act of the mind by which it
turns its view back upon itself and its opera-

tions to consider its own ideas attentively; it compares, weighs, and matures them. It is on this act that depend the sources of genius and the perfection of reasoning.

Q. What is the composition of ideas?

A. The mind contemplating its ideas by the aid of reflection collects them, recapitulates them, retrenches from them all that is superfluous, and forms from them a more simple and intelligible whole.

A simple idea is one that is distinct from every other idea; such are the ideas of affirmation, negation, and of unity. The complex idea on the contrary, is one which, under a simple form, includes several other ideas: such are the ideas of a clock, of an armillary sphere, and of the human body.

Q. Can simple ideas be defined?

A. No; because the definition is an explana tion and development of an idea; now simple ideas can neither be explained nor developed, because they are not composed, and we can explain only what is composed; for instance: We may define anger, " an impetuous movement of trouble of mind and body, occasioned by the presence of a disagreeable idea, or by a formal opposition to our will;" therefore, we can not define simple ideas.

Q. What is abstraction?

A. It is an operation of the mind, by which we retrench the properties of an object, or the attributes of a being, in order to examine it with greater facility.

Q. Is this a useful mental operation?

A. It is not only useful, but also very necessary; for the attention is proportionately weaker as it reposes upon a greater number of objects; and as sometimes, it can not embrace them all at once, it becomes necessary to retrench the accessory ideas in order to fix the attention solely upon the principal ideas. For, according to a universally received adage, the sense that we apply to several objects at the same time, becomes less for each one of them.

Q. How do we form universal ideas by means of abstraction?

A. It is by retrenching from an object all the attributes which particularly belong to it and which especially distinguish it, in order to consider it under a general view which agrees with several objects of the same nature. If, for example, I think of a person whom I know particularly well, all his qualities, good or bad, are immediately retraced in my imagination; I can see his clothes, his deportment, his gait, &c. However, if I wish to form a universal idea, by means of abstraction, I retrench all the ideas which were connected with this person, to consider only his humanity; now, the idea of humanity is applicable to all persons, as it is applicable to the person who is at that moment the object of my thought; hence I have formed a universal idea.

Q. What is the comparison of ideas?

A. It is an operation by which the mind, reflecting upon itself, gives its attention successively to the different ideas that it proposes to examine. Sometimes it considers them all together, sometimes it examines them separately, in order to find the relations that they may have to each other, or to discover their differences. Those which have a relation to each other are those which, at the same time, may suit the same subject, such are the ideas of extension and mobility, which at the same time, may be attributed to one and the same subject. Incompatible ideas are those which contradict one another and which we can not suppose present at the same time; for example, the idea of calmness and the idea of anger, can not exist at the same time in the same person.

Q. What is the distinction of ideas?

A. It is an act of the mind by which it compares its ideas and distinguishes them separately,

2*

one from the other. It is on this operation that their clearness depends. We say that an idea is clear, when it represents its object in such a manner as to cause it to be well understood, whatever it may be. We say that an idea is distinct, when it shows its object in such a manner, that it can not be confounded with any other object.

FIRST PROPOSITION.

Every idea is distinct.—Ideas represent in objects, similar properties as similar, and different properties as different ; for ideas represent objects such as they are in themselves, since they represent the nature of those same objects: thus, all ideas are distinct.

Q. All ideas are not distinct, because on seeing an object, on examining it, we may confound it with another. For instance, if you are shown a foreign animal similar to another animal which you have formerly seen, you confound the two, and you think that the new animal is the same one that you saw before. So also, if you were shown a multiform figure, you might confound it with another figure also multiform, which would differ from the first one merely in having one side more or less. Therefore, may I not conclude that all ideas are not distinct, since they do not cause us to distinguish one object from another with exact precision ?

A. 1st. On seeing an animal, the idea that I acquire represents to me properties which may also belong to an animal which I have never seen. When then I see that animal (which I have not previously seen), my mind acquires anew the idea of those same properties; and as these two ideas represent the same thing, it is not astonishing that I can not distinguish the second animal from the first, since I am only acquainted with the properties that are common to both; so that, properly speaking, I have not an exact idea of either of those animals, but only the idea of two animals that have common properties. But if I had the idea of the particular properties found in each one of them, or if I had the idea of each one in particular, I should have no trouble in distinguishing one from the other.

2d. When I compare the idea of one multiform figure with another that is exactly like it with the exception of only one side, I distinguish clearly one figure from the other figure, however I could not recognize them separately without a mature examination, because my first idea was that of a *multiform* figure for the two objects, and not that of a figure of a *certain* number of sides. But because we can not always distinguish clearly the external objects which make an impression on our senses, it does not follow that the internal objects, which are the true objects of our ideas, are not represented in a manner perfectly distinct to our minds.

SECOND PROPOSITION.

Every idea is clear.—By a clear idea we mean one that makes known to us perfectly the nature of the object of our idea. Now, every idea makes its object known as it is; for every idea is perceived by the mind, and besides, it represents its object such as it is; thus every idea makes its object known in a distinct manner, therefore every idea is clear.

Q. If every idea were clear, the objects that we see would be reflected immediately in our mind such as they are; now, they are not represented in our mind such as they really are, because if I see a lion at a distance, I directly conceive the idea of an object, yet without knowing certainly what it is; that idea is therefore not clear, hence is it not wrong to say that every idea is clear?

A. To solve this difficulty, it is sufficient to avoid confounding the idea with the judgment. I ask myself what was my first idea; and I find that this first idea was of a body. It is only *after* I have judged that this body could be or must be that of a wolf or an ox that I am deceived;— but it is only in my judgment formed concerning the body that furnished my first idea; now the first idea did not deceive me, this is clear; hence we can not conclude from this objection, that the proposition " every idea is clear " is false, since the objection itself proves in favor of the proposition.

Q. However, do we not often hear it said, and do we not ourselves often *assert*, " *I have only a confused idea of that.*" " *My ideas are confused.*" *That man can not render an account of his ideas, they are so confused*; now whatever is generally accepted, or generally admitted, becomes an axiom; an axiom is a principle so evident that we can not contest it without exposing ourselves to the taunt of idiocy. If, therefore, our objection is based upon an axiom, it will be impossible for you to prove that every idea is clear, hence, must we not conclude that the proposition, " every idea is clear," must be false?

A. When an idea represents some properties of an object, without making the object sufficiently known to us, it may be styled confused, as respects that object, but not in reference to the properties that it represents. Strictly speaking,

an idea is neither clear nor confused in respect
to what it does not represent; but we style it
confused, in order to denote that it does not represent a sufficient number of the properties of
the object to make the object well known to us.
Now, in this sense, the idea of the body, as a
whole, is confused, but it does not follow that the
idea, considered abstractly, is confused; hence it
is not just to conclude that the proposition,
"Every idea is clear," is false.

Q. Into how many classes are ideas divided?

A. Ideas are divided into different classes,
according to the manner in which they are considered, whether with regard to themselves, their
origin, the things that they represent, or the
manner in which the things are represented.

1. Ideas, when considered in reference to
themselves are divided into ideas of sensation
and ideas of reflection. An idea of perception
is the perception of an object represented; and
an idea of reflection is the consciousness of that
perception.

2. Ideas, considered in reference to their
origin, are subdivided into three kinds: *innate*
ideas; the *adventitious* ideas, or those which
occur fortuitously; and *factitious* ideas.

Innate ideas are those which God has graven
within us from the instant of our birth; such

is the idea of God himself, for it has been discovered in several instances that man, at his birth, brings with him the idea of a Supreme Being.* Many savages, drawn from the depths of the forest, who had never heard of God, nevertheless entertained a very correct idea of Him, because they rendered a species of worship to an Omnipotent Being. This is a truth sufficiently proved, and it is even one of the most irresistible arguments that can be employed against the Atheist.

Adventitious *ideas*, are those that are communicated to the mind through the medium of the senses, when the presence of any body strikes them; such is the idea of the sun, or of a flower.

Factitious ideas are those which are formed from the primitive ideas already existing in the mind. Thus, the idea of a *golden mountain* is factitious, because it is composed of the idea of a mountain and the idea of gold.

Ideas, considered in reference to their origin, may be also divided into those of pure intelligence, imagination, and perception of sensations. Pure intelligence is that sort of perception which represents an object to the mind,

---

* It may be well to inform the beginner that the idea of infinity can only come from revelation.—[Trans.

without the aid of the senses. It teaches us to know God, to know ourselves, and to recognize and admit the mathematical properties of bodies, such as the equality of the radii of a circle.

The Imagination is a perception by which we represent to ourselves objects under a sensible form, without employing our exterior senses. Thus, when the eyes are closed, we may imagine that we see the sun, with its glorious rays; or a rainbow, adorned with the luster of a thousand hues.

The perception of sensations is that which creates ideas in the mind, by meeting objects which fall under our senses. For example: I am not thinking of my book; I perceive it lying on the table, and immediately the idea of a book is reflected in my mind.

Q. Are the ideas that are communicated to us through the medium of the senses always correct in respect to the objects which they represent?

A. No, they sometimes contradict each other, for example: if a long pole be plunged into clear water, it appears bent, to the most attentive observer; but if one passes the hand along the pole, the pole will be found to be straight. In such a case the understanding must decide, because the two ideas can not destroy each other; and, after examining the causes that may produce this effect, the first judgment must be retracted. We may conclude, from the example of the pole in the clear water, that our senses are apt to lead us into the commission of numerous errors. But a modest mind will never shrink from retracting an error as soon as it has discovered its mistake; it will endure reproof, patiently listen to the opposite reasoning, and, when convinced, will not consider that it degrades itself by surrendering to the correct reasoning of its adversary.*

*Although foreign to the subject we are treating, we can not refrain from presenting an instance of sincere humility, which may serve as a model—presuming the digression will be easily pardoned on account of the appropriateness of the example.

The illustrious Archbishop of Cambrai disputed a long time in defense of his doctrine of pure love, against the luminous observations of the learned Bossuet; so long as the case remained without decision, M. de Fenélon supported his cause with firmness; but as soon as the ecclesiastical authority of Rome decided that his doctrine was erroneous, he, with a submission of which none but a great mind is capable, ordered the pernicious book that contained this doctrine to be burned, and thus left to the church a durable monument of his obedience, as well as of his defeat.

Never suffer yourselves to be dazzled by impressions which flatter, or discouraged by those that displease; but always yield to reflection, aided by sound judgment, and then the oracle of Holy Writ will be realized in you. Isaiah xi. 2:—"And the Spirit of the Lord shall rest upon him; he shall not judge according to the sight of the eyes, nor reprove according to the hearing of the ears."

3. Ideas, considered in reference to their object, are divided into ideas of substance, ideas of mode, and ideas of substance modified. The idea of substance is of that which exists by itself, as a circle, a tree, a triangle, &c. The idea of mode is that which represents one object contained in another object, as color, form, &c.; because those objects can not subsist alone, but must be included in another body. That which presents itself with its mode, or accident, we style idea of substance modified; such are the ideas of a red book, a learned man.

Ideas, considered in reference to their object, are also divided into singular, particular, and universal.

The singular idea is one which represents but one thing, or one determinate idea, whether single, complex, or compound. Such is the idea which represents to us one person, as John, or James. The object determined by the singular idea is called an *individual*.

The *particular idea* represents one indeterminate individual, as some one, a man, &c.

A *universal idea* is that which is applicable to all the individuals of a class.

CHAPTER II.

All the means that we employ to manifest our thoughts, are called signs.

We will first speak of signs in general, and then of signs in particular.

ARTICLE FIRST.

OF SIGNS IN GENERAL.

Question. What is a sign in general?

Answer. A sign in general is that which makes something known to us. It always awakens two ideas within us, first the idea of itself, and then the idea of the thing it signifies.

It is employed to represent things past, present, and future. In the first case it is styled *commemorative*, and in the second *representative*, and in the third *prognostic*. The commemorative sign recalls past events; thus, the column in the Place Vendome in Paris, recalls an epoch in the

history of France, during which her astonishing
valor triumphed over her enemies.   The representative sign discloses to us what is passing
at the very instant in which we perceive it;
thus a fierce countenance, earnest gestures, and
an irritated tone of voice prove to us that a man
is angry.   The prognostic sign makes known future things; for instance, when the sky is ob-
scured by thick, dark clouds, we prognosticate
that it will soon rain.   By certain signs also, we
recognize that a sick person will soon die.

Signs are either natural, or artificial, that is
arbitrary.

Q. What is a natural sign ?

A. It is one that by itself, and its own nature,
denotes the object that it represents; thus tears
are a sign of sadness, and laughter is a sign of joy.

Q. What is an artificial or arbitrary sign ?

A. It is one that derives its significance merely
from the value that men have assigned to it by
common consent, at least in those places where
it is adopted.   It depends wholly upon human
institutions, for men may abolish it, or replace it
by any other sign.   Thus, in some countries of
France, a branch of a tree placed above the door
of a house, signifies that wine is for sale there.
In some boarding schools, a blue ribbon and a
medal signify that the pupil who wears them is

diligent in her studies, and submissive to the rules of the establishment.

Signs are either certain or uncertain.

Q. What is a certain sign ?

A. A certain sign is one that has such a close connection with the thing signified, that it is impossible for it to lead us into error; thus smoke is a certain sign of fire; respiration is a certain sign of animal life.

Q. What is an uncertain sign ?

A. An uncertain sign is one that only gives us probabilities. For example: a young person prays; it is probable that it is because she is pious; but the hypocrite prays too; the sign of praying alone is therefore insufficient to prove that the young person is pious—because she might very easily be a hypocrite.

A person eats meat on days of abstinence; it is a certain sign that she does not observe the laws of the Church; but it is not a certain sign that she is committing sin; because, she may have obtained a dispensation on just grounds.

ARTICLE SECOND.

OF THE SIGNS OF OUR THOUGHTS.

As men were formed to live in society, they

were forced to create means to render the communication of their thoughts easy; for thought
being produced in the mind can not be expressed
exteriorly without the aid of signs.

Q. What signs have men invented whereby
to manifest their thoughts ?

A. Three : 1. Gestures ; 2. Language ; 3
Writing.

OF GESTURE.

Question. What is gesture ?

Answer. Gesture is the expression of thought
by various movements of the members of the
body.

Consider the pantomimists, whose art consists
in representing entire dramas by gesture alone;
consider the dumb, who, on account of their in-
ability to speak, succeed so perfectly with gestures as to excite the spectator to sympathize
with them, and even to experience the same
emotions as those they represent; for there is
no shade of thought so nice that it can not be
expressed by the motion of the eyes, mouth, or
head, or by a movement of the hand.

It is chiefly among the Orientals that the imagination seeks for images, and for action in discourse. Thus we read in the 19th chapter of
Jeremiah, that the holy prophet appeared among

those enthusiastic people, loaded with chains, and bearing earthen vessels in his hands, when he went to reproach them with their iniquities, and exhort them to be converted to the Lord.

OF THE VOICE, OR OF SPEECH.

Question. Define speech ?

Answer. It is an articulate sound, uttered with the intention of making something known. We call it *articulate*, because it is, as it were, separated into articulations by syllables ; in this respect it differs from the sounds uttered by brutes. I say to make known something, that is to express an idea ; because to the word is attached the idea meant to be conveyed. There are, it is true, certain birds which appear to enounce articulate sounds, as parrots, ravens, magpies, &c. ; but these birds attach no idea to the words they utter ; they have no merit except that of repeating certain articulate sounds which have been taught them, and sometimes with great difficulty ; therefore it is not the idea that the word conveys that has made an impression on their brain, but simply and positively sound alone.

Q. Is speech an arbitrary sign ?

A. No ; speech is a Divine gift : God bestowed it upon man, to assist him to live in society with his kind, and to distinguish him from other creatures over whom he was established the sovereign, and that these creatures might be subject to him.

Q. Are the words employed in language arbitrary signs?

A. Yes; words are arbitrary signs, because they were invented by men. We find the proof in the great variety of tongues which exist on the surface of the globe. All the signs or words which they adopt are purely arbitrary, since, to signify the same thing, there are as many different terms as there are different languages; thus the word God, in English, is used to express the Supreme Being, Theos in Greek, Deus in Latin, Dios in Spanish, Iddio in Italian, Gott in German, Bog in Polish.

If words were not arbitrary, they would have such an affinity with thought, that, on changing them, the thought would be no longer the same: now, men change their modes of expression and invent new ones almost daily; and this fact led Horace to say:—

" A multitude of words, now considered obsolete, will be presented anew with honor, and the greater number of words now in vogue will, in their turn, be considered antiquated, and will sink into oblivion.

" So custom wills it, for custom or usage is

the great master and sovereign arbiter of language."

OF WRITING.

Speech having been given to men to enable them to communicate their ideas, they used this inestimable benefit of their Creator so long as they dwelt in the same locality. But ere long, the human family becoming very numerous, it was found necessary for them to separate, to seek new abodes, and thus great distances interrupted communication. But those thus divided were relatives and friends; alliances had been contracted among the various families, and these families soon increased so as to form nations, with distinct customs and separate laws. The necessity of exchanging the productions of one country for those of others, gave rise to commerce; then it became requisite to establish connections and means of communication, and this was first accomplished by messengers; but as such a method was very slow, as well as extremely difficult and expensive, the genius of man summoned all its energies to contrive a more prompt and advantageous mode; and discovered one in the art of writing.

It is pretended that Cadmus first taught this ingenious art to the Phenicians. It is un-

3

known to what people the invention of the
Alphabet should be attributed. The Hebrew,
Phenician, Syriac, Chaldaic, Arabic, Grecian,
and Latin alphabets have all probably the same
origin, for the analogy between the forms of the
letters is very striking.

Q. Had men any means of communicating
thought previous to the invention of the alphabet ?

A. Yes; they began by employing certain
signs, to which they gave the title *hieroglyphics.*

Q. In what country were these signs principally held in esteem ?

A. In Egypt, where the priests were the de-
positaries and the interpreters of this science.

Q. Explain the nature of hieroglyphics more
fully.

A. Hieroglyphics, as we have said above, are
certain signs or pictures, by means of which some
early nations, and particularly the Egyptian,
expressed ideas.

The Mexicans also employed them to write
their laws and record their annals, so as to trans-
mit them to posterity. With the aid of painting,
these people depicted sensible objects under appropriate figures, and employed special characters
for representing invisible things. Gradually,
this rude art, which required enormous volumes,

improved; instead of painting an entire history, it was found sufficient to inscribe the chief circumstances of an historical event to signify the whole. Two hands, one holding a bow, and the other a shield, represented a battle; the bow denoted an attack, the shield a defense or resistance. An eye placed above a rod or scepter, signified the all-seeing Providence of God. A hand was emblematic of supreme power and justice; a circle represented eternity; a serpent, treachery, &c., &c.

In the lapse of time they substituted for these pictures certain sketches or outlines that were easier to engrave; each drawing had a particular conventional meaning. To these improved drawings the name letters was given; of letters, words were formed by common consent, and thus the art of writing was invented.

SECOND PART.

JUDGMENT.

Judgment must be considered :—1. In reference to its existence within the mind, when it is called *judgment.* 2. In reference to its expression in words when it is called *proposition.*

CHAPTER I.

OF JUDGMENT CONSIDERED IN REFERENCE TO ITS EXISTENCE WITHIN THE MIND.

ARTICLE FIRST.

Question. What is Judgment?

Answer. Judgment is an act of the mind, by which we affirm or deny some circumstance concerning another thing.

When I say " *God is good,*" I affirm concerning God that He is good; and hence I have formed a judgment, because, in the act of judging, we compare two known ideas; therefore, the mind is capable of entertaining two ideas, two perceptions, at the same time; if not, how can it institute comparisons?

If, on the contrary, I affirm that a triangle is not a square, I form a negative judgment; for I deny that the triangle has the property of squareness. But to arrive at this conclusion, it was necessary for me first to observe the form of the triangle, and then the form of the square; and, judging that these two figures have not the same shape, the same property, I conclude that the triangle is not square.

Therefore, judgment is the result of a comparison formed within the mind.

PROPOSITION.

Judgment is a simple act of the mind. This act consists either in uniting or separating ideas; for if I say: " *The grief that I experience is great,*" my judgment is formed in respect to an interior sensation. Now, this union or this separation is something indivisible and simple. When I say " *God is good,*" I unite the idea of God with the idea of goodness by a simple act, which is not composed of the two ideas that I thus united; thus judgment comprises only affirmation or negation; hence the judgment is a simple act of the mind.

The proposition differs from the judgment, in

that the proposition comprises the subject, the attribute, and the verb, or copula. For instance, in the proposition, " *God is good*," the subject is *God*, the attribute or predicate, is *good*, and the copula or verb *is*, connects the predicate with the subject. Thus, the proposition contains several parts; but the judgment, as it is in the mind, consists simply in affirmation or negation; it is consequently a simple act, which unites or separates the ideas which are not the substance of the judgment, but which must be considered the substance on which the judgment is exercised.

Q. But every object is composed of its own substance; therefore the judgment is composed of the ideas that it unites or separates, and consequently it is not a simple act of the mind.

A. If, by saying that every object is composed of its own substance, we understand that each object *is what it is*, in that sense, the judgment has a substance which is not distinct from itself, and which is merely a simple act of the mind, that unites ideas or separates them. If, on the contrary, we pretend thereby that every object is composed of material parts like bodies, or even of *parts* that are not material, this is false; for it is evident that our ideas are not material. Now, what is not material can not be composed of parts; hence it is false to say that our *ideas are*

composed of their own substance. So much the
more, because our ideas originate in the soul,
which is itself immaterial, and can no more produce material objects than it can be produced by
matter; for if we admit the principle, " *Every
object is composed of its own substance,*" it would
follow that the soul of man is material, that its
Creator is also material, which would be an
inconceivable absurdity ; for neither blind chance
nor blind matter could have created the human
soul, the essence of light.

ARTICLE SECOND.

OF THE EFFICIENT CAUSE OF THE JUDGMENT.

Question. To which of the faculties does judgment belong?

Answer. Philosophers are divided in their
opinions on this subject ; some of them pretend
that it belongs to the will. We shall adopt this
view (which seems to us the most correct), for
the judgment being perfectly free, it must be an
act of the will controlled by the understanding.

PROPOSITION.

Judgment is an act of the will, rather than an
act of the understanding.

Q. How do you prove this proposition ?

A. The Judgment is always voluntary and free; for we may deduce an affirmative or negative judgment, without any one being able to prevent us doing so; now this act appertains rather to the will, which is an active power of the soul, than to the understanding, which is a passive power of the soul.

Q. But might we not say that the judgment belongs neither to the understanding, which is unable to see the agreement or disagreement of ideas, nor to the will which is only susceptible of desire, hatred, love or command ?

A. The power of feeling pleasure and pain is widely different from the power of knowing and willing; so also, the power of judging differs from all the other faculties of the soul. Therefore, we must attribute judgment to the faculty of deciding, which is none other than the will.

ARTICLE THIRD.

OF THE MOTIVES OF OUR JUDGMENTS.

Question. What do you mean by the motive of a judgment ?

Answer. It is the *reason* that inclines the mind to conclude; and that *reason* I call motive, because it seems to move or excite the mind to act, and cause it to form a judgment, either affirmative or negative.

Q. How many sorts of motive are there?

A. Two; the certain motive and the uncertain motive.

Q. What is a certain motive?

A. It is one which has a necessary connection with the truth of the judgment which it excites.

Q. What is an uncertain motive?

A. It is one that is not so connected with the verity of the judgment as not to exclude all fear of error.

Q. How many kinds of certainty are there?

A. Three; metaphysical certainty, physical certainty, and moral certainty.

Q. What is metaphysical certainty?

A. Metaphysical certainty is that which produces the idea and even the nature of things, in such a manner that in any hypothesis whatsoever it can not be otherwise.

The following propositions are metaphysical:

The whole is greater than any of its parts.

The Creator is more powerful than his creature.

A part is less than the whole.

Q. What is a physical certainty?

A. A physical certainty is one which is founded on the ordinary laws of nature, whose order can not be inverted except by miracle. It is by a physical certainty that I believe that the sun will rise to-morrow, to give light to our globe. It is also by physical certainty that astronomers calculate so exactly the phases of the moon.

Q. What do you understand by a moral certainty?

A. By moral certainty I mean, that which is founded upon the moral constitution, and upon certain general laws which control the mind and understanding. These laws afford as much certainty as the immutable laws of physics and metaphysics.

Men also consider as motives of their judgments, consciousness, evidence, revelation, the testimony of the senses, and human testimony.

These various motives are the sources of two others, memory and analogy.

Q. What is Consciousness?

A. Consciousness consists in that kind of perception by which the mind is apprised of its present state. It is consciousness that causes us to feel grief, joy, fear, hope, remorse, and interior peace. It may, therefore, be also styled conscience (which signifies knowledge). Hence, when we have committed any fault, that conscience or knowledge of it, that we have within us, ceases not to reproach us with the fault we have committed.

There have been men so insincere or so dishonest as to deny the existence of conscience, but it was only to endeavor to procure a false peace to their own consciences which were stung with remorse.

PROPOSITION.

Consciousness is a motive of judging which is metaphysically certain. We have said above that a motive metaphysically certain is one that is founded on the nature of things, so that it is impossible for it to deceive us in any hypothesis whatever. Consciousness is founded on the nature of things, it can not deceive us; therefore it is a metaphysical certainty.

If consciousness could deceive us, it would *be* and *not be*, because the affections would exist and would not be found in the soul. They would exist in the sense that the *soul* would feel them, which could not happen unless they reside in the soul itself; they would not be, or exist, because they would conduct the soul into error, which could never happen if they resided within it.

Therefore, the mind can not be deceived by

consciousness, because consciousness can not *be*, and *not be*, at the same time ; therefore, consciousness, in any hypothesis whatever, has a veritable connection with truth ; hence, it is a motive of judgment, metaphysically certain.

Q. What is Evidence ?

A. Evidence is a clear perception of the agreement or disagreement of ideas with each other ; thus, I say it is evident that two and two make four, because I perceive clearly and distinctly the agreement that exists between twice two and four. For the same reason, when I behold the rays of the sun, I say, " The sun shines."

PROPOSITION.

Evidence is a motive of judgment, metaphysically certain. A motive metaphysically certain is one that can not deceive in any hypothesis whatever. Now, evidence can not deceive in any hypothesis soever, for it can not at the same time *exist* and *not exist*. If the perception of a clear and obvious idea could deceive us, it *would be* and *not be*, and as what is obvious and distinct really exists, evidence, being a clear and obvious perception, can not deceive us. Therefore evidence is a metaphysically certain motive of our judgments.

Q. What is Revelation ?

A. By Revelation is meant, an exterior mani-festation of some truth, which God has deigned to impart to men.

There have been unbelievers who have dared to deny the possibility of Divine Revelation; this need not surprise us, as there are men so impious as to deny the existence of God him-self. But these individuals do not believe what they profess, for if you watch them closely, you will often surprise them betraying themselves; that is, you will find them practicing certain acts which prove that in spite of themselves they are obliged to admit that there is a God. The impious man hath said in his heart: " There is no God !" He has *said* it, and he would like to persuade himself of it; but as every thing within him proves the contrary, his pride is forced to bend before the innate sense of Deity.

A sentiment similar to that of the Atheist, has induced certain philosophers to deny the pos-sibility of Revelation; but how can man dare deny God a power which he himself has re-ceived from the Divine bounty ? How absurd, to deny that the Supreme Being is able to mani-fest His will, while feeble man, the creature of His omnipotence enjoys this faculty ?

FIRST PROPOSITION.

Divine Revelation is an infallible motive of judgment in the supernatural order.

As Divine Revelation is the testimony of God himself, who is sovereignly true, and can neither deceive nor be deceived, therefore Divine Revelation is an infallible motive of judgment in the supernatural order.

SECOND PROPOSITION.

Divine Revelation was necessary for man, to instruct him in things that surpass his intelligence.

Divine Intelligence surpasses human intelligence infinitely, and consequently possesses a far greater number of truths, and of a superior order. Now, in that boundless field of knowledge which surpasses the intellect of man, there are some truths which are advantageous for him to know, that he may secure his eternal salvation. God, who is a Being of infinite benevolence, manifested to man those truths which he is obliged to believe in order to be saved; therefore, Divine Revelation was absolutely necessary to make known to us those mysteries which surpass our finite intelligence.

OF THE TESTIMONY OF THE SENSES.

Question. What is meant by the testimony of the senses ?

Answer. If I consider the testimony of the senses as sensation, I answer that it is an affection of the soul excited within us by the presence of an object, or by a sound, or by an agreeable or disagreeable recital ; thence spring the various sensations that we experience, according to our relations with different objects or with different sounds.

If, on the contrary, I consider the testimony of the senses as the relation of the sensation, I reply, that it is that natural propensity which inclines us to ascribe our sensations to the exterior objects which produced them.

It seems useless to prove that the testimony of the senses is a certain motive of our judgment; we will merely say that several philosophers have denied the existence of the bodies that produce our sensations ; they have even been so extravagant as to say that heat is not in fire, but in ourselves. To confound them, it will be sufficient to quote the words of the illustrious Father Buffier, S. J. :

" I have often wondered why Descartes and Malebranche, with their disciples, vaunted, as a rare discovery of their philosophy, that heat is in ourselves, and not in fire; whilst the generality of men find that heat exists both in fire and in ourselves. ... Of what is there question? solely of the poverty of language, which causes a confused idea of heat. The word *heat* expresses equally well two things, which, in truth, have some relation or analogy, but which are really very different; namely, first, the *sensation* of heat which we experience within us; secondly, the disposition that is in fire to produce the sensation of heat. But, once more, is the subject as important as those new philosophers would have us think? Did ever any genuine error on the subject exist? Who, among even the commonest intellects, ever dreamt that there exists in fire a sensation of heat such as we experience?"

OF HUMAN TESTIMONY.

As men do not all reside in one place, and do not all live at the same period of time, we can only be informed of the actions and events which have occurred at a distance from us, and at a remote epoch, by the testimony of our fellow-beings, who either witnessed them, or heard them related by others. If the events are important and greatly to our advantage to know, we desire that the testimony concerning them should be worthy of credit; then, in order that their testimony may be an infallible motive of judgment, and that it may produce absolute certainty, it becomes necessary that the events related be possible and important, for men are only interested in what concerns their present and future lot, their own fortune, and the fate of empires. The facts or events narrated must also have a necessary connection with posterior events, so as more readily to explain their existence. Thus the propagation of the Christian religion necessarily supposes the miracles of our Lord and of His Apostles. The facts must also be admitted by those to whom it imports most that they be denied, or at least that those enemies be not able to offer any solid motive for contesting them. Finally, these circumstances and events must be narrated not merely by one individual, but by several witnesses, who were incapable either of deceiving or of being deceived.

Yet, there have been men who professed to doubt every thing; and our modern philosophers, finding it convenient to follow their example, have raised and maintained the most absurd doubts concerning the existence of facts, more than sufficiently proved by the *testimony* of a long line of centuries: for instance, they

pretend to doubt the authenticity of the Holy
Scriptures. We can refute their doubts with
the following article borrowed from "Le
Dictionnaire Encyclopédique. Art., 'Certi-
tude':"—

"How is it possible to suspect that a book has
been forged, when we find it quoted by ancient
writers, and founded upon the testimony of an
unbroken chain of witnesses, all agreeing together, especially when this chain begins at the
time in which it is said that the book was written, and only finishes with ourselves? Again, if
there were no books that quoted this book as
belonging to such an author or to such authors,
to prove its authenticity, it would be sufficient
for me to know that it has been handed down to
me as the production of such an author, by an
uninterrupted oral tradition, from its own epoch
down to myself and upon several collateral lines.
Besides, there are, in these books, works that interest whole kingdoms and entire nations, and
hence never could have been forged. Some contain the annals of the nation and its titles; others
its laws and customs; others contain their religion. The more men in general are accused of
superstition, the more we must allow they keep
their eyes open on whatever concerns their religion. A whole nation could never be ignorant

of the origin of a book which regulates its belief
and determines all its hopes."

In truth, to deny the authenticity of a book so
widely spread abroad as is the Bible, and pre-
served so carefully by those even whose highest
interest would lead them to deny its existence,
may be considered as ridiculous as to attempt to
deny that the emperor Augustus lived in Rome,
or that Louis XIV. was king of France. In vain
would they found their doubts upon the *darkness*
and obscurity of the numerous ages that have
elapsed since the writing or compiling of that
sublime Book, for *time*, says an author, has ever
been considered the parent of truth; it draws it
from obscurity when it is hidden, and gives it
stability when it is uncertain and doubtful; on
the contrary, it suppresses Falsehood, when it
adorns itself inappropriately with the colors of
Truth. With time we examine, discuss, and
penetrate truth. Whatever was capable of deceiving the heated imaginations of ordinary
minds, by a concurrence of various circumstances favorable to error, has no longer the
same effect when those circumstances cease to
exist; posterity easily reforms the false or erroneous judgments of its predecessors; the lapse
of years and of centuries dissipates the mists of
fables and chimeras; truth comes forth, it pre-

vails, and when a fact has passed the ordeal
of several ages, when it has maintained itself in
the mind and memory of men as certain and in-
dubitable, notwithstanding the diversity of the
judgments and the discordant interests of so
many nations; when it has endured the numerous and multiform attacks of the spirit of contra-
diction (which reappears in every succeeding
age), it must be allowed that such a fact has
attained so high a degree of certainty that nothing can disturb it.

As the Christian religion is founded upon
supernatural facts that we can only know by
human testimony, unbelievers have spared no
pains to excite doubts in respect to these facts,
and then to contest positively their existence;
they even go so far as to declare that, if all
Paris were to affirm that a man was raised
from the dead, they would not believe it. But is
it not absurd to say that the testimony of a mil-
lion of men is not sufficient to establish the in-
contestability of a fact? Is it not actually re-
fusing to submit to evidence? for, adds the same
author, the witnesses have not all the same passions and interests; many among them have no
acquaintance with each other; numbers never
saw each other; how, then, could there possibly
be connivance among them? A conspiracy of

such a vast city as Paris, formed without motive
or interest, between people who do not know
each other, is more difficult to believe than that a
man was raised from the dead. The resurrection
is opposed to the laws of the physical world;
such a conspiracy would be opposed to the laws
of the moral world. A prodigy would be requisite for each, with this difference, that the latter
would be far greater than the former. That God
should raise a dead man to life to manifest His
goodness or to set a seal upon some great truth,
I admit, would suffice to induce me to acknowl-
edge His omnipotence; but that God should
overturn the order of society, suspend the action
of moral causes, and force men, by a miraculous
impression, to violate all their ordinary rules
of conduct, and that merely to deceive one
simple, private individual (I confess, indeed,
His infinite power), appears to me contrary
to the wisdom that guides His divine operations; therefore, it is more possible that a dead
man should rise again, than that all Paris
should conspire to deceive me concerning this
miracle.

Memory is also a certain motive of judgment,
because, if we have witnessed a circumstance of
importance, or have heard it related, the mind is
so impressed by what it has seen or heard, that we

not only retain the substance of the details, but also every circumstance of interest.

Q. But can the memory be a reliable motive of judgment, since nothing is more frequently heard than—"I have no memory, my memory has deceived me?"

A. It is true that we very often try to recall a circumstance without being able to succeed; but in such cases memory fails, but memory does not leads us into error.

The last certain motive of judgment, is analogy.

Q. What is Analogy?

A. It is a certain concatenation of facts having a certain relation, resemblance or identity; thus medicinal plants are only employed by reason of their analogy. However, it can not be denied that reasoning by analogy is subject to numerous errors; but if the relations between objects are obvious, their traits of resemblance perfectly similar, then analogy becomes a certain motive of judgment.

ARTICLE FOURTH.

OF THE ERRORS TO WHICH THE JUDGMENTS OF MEN ARE SUBJECT, AND THE MEANS OF AVOID-ING THEM.

When we exercise our judgment we are liable to fall into many mistakes; these mistakes may proceed from judging with too much precipitation, from the influence of prejudice, from an excited imagination, which gives a false view of things, or from ignorance, all of which prevent us from discerning motives, causes, circumstances and their effects.

Question. What is Precipitation?

Answer. It is forming a judgment too hastily, and with levity, concerning some action or event that we have not taken time or pains to examine maturely.

This defect is very general, especially among young pupils, who answer questions without discernment, and according to the first thought that presents itself to the mind. The inconveniences arising from precipitation are numerous and grave, I may add dangerous. A young person who does not reflect before forming her conclusions may not only pass for silly and ignorant (though possessing wit and information); but precipitation will prove a source of many trials and difficulties during life, because she will lightly credit all that is told her, she will even report it: she will not perceive the consequences of her words, and may thus at times injure the reputation of her companions; and from this might arise enmities which would only terminate with life. To herself personally, precipitation will prove *seriously* injurious and affect her whole life ; for when one has the reputation of levity, sensible persons will distrust her, and perhaps even avoid her society. To prevent all these vexatious consequences, and the dangers to which this defect may expose them, young persons should always take time to examine and consider before coming to a conclusion; they should distrust their own *judgment*, and if they meet with a difficulty, never hesitate to consult persons more enlightened and more' experienced than themselves.

It is chiefly in conversation that we judge rashly or precipitately. If evil is spoken of another, the accusation is unhesitatingly credited, then reported to others, and thus the unfortunate person becomes the subject of either detraction or calumny. Before giving credence to a rumor, consider whether the narrator may not be a habitual detractor or even falsifier; and even though she be irreproachable on these two points, examine of whom the ill is spoken ; what are her habits. morals, position, and religous principles; and if you continue to find resemblance, probability, nay, truth itself, I still say to you : "Believe not !" First, because we should avoid "thinking evil," according to St. Paul; and according to St. Francis of Sales, reputation is like broadcloth.

If you examine it on the *right side*, you will find
it soft, smooth, and free from any inequality, but
if you examine it on the *wrong side*, you will discover roughness and various other defects. It
is advisable to shun company in which evil is
spoken of others, or in which their defects are
ridiculed, and it would be well to remember the
following homely illustration : " That the wicked
resemble flies, which when running over a body,
never stop but at its wounds."

Q. What are Prejudices?

A. Prejudices are judgments passed before
we have examined all the circumstances of both
sides of a case on which we are called to decide :
therefore prejudices are always unreasonable.
Prejudice is the source of superstition, which
leads men into a multitude of practices, each
one of which is more unreasonable than the other.
These two defects arise from listening to old women's tales, which are calculated to affect a feeble
and untutored imagination.

Prejudice, says the author of *"Recherches sur
la Religion,"* is opposed to *certainty* and not to
truth. Therefore it is not precisely an error, and
it would be reasoning inaccurately to say : "such
an opinion is a prejudice, hence it is false."

When we consider prejudices as the source of
error, we mean to speak only of those, which

though false in their object, are nevertheless treated as general and demonstrated truths.

The sources of prejudices are, that *natural propensity* of man to believe on indifferent motives, the necessity of believing something, and indolence in examining.

The principal causes of our prejudices are: 1st.' The senses and the imagination; 2d. A natural inclination to believe on the authority of our parents, our teachers, our friends, and of those who are of the same nation, or commonwealth; 3d, and finally, sloth.

Bossuet, the celebrated Bishop of Meaux, in his Abridgment on Philosophy, says: "The cause of wrong judgment is inconsiderateness, or want of reflection, called otherwise precipitation. To precipitate one's judgment (or as we commonly say to judge rashly), is to believe or to judge before knowing. This happens from pride, impatience, or conclusions made too hastily, or without due examination of both sides of a question.

" From pride, for pride inclines us to presume that we can comprehend the most difficult things without waiting to examine them. Thus we judge promptly, are attached to our way of thinking, and are unwilling to examine lest we should be forced to admit that we have been mistaken.

" From impatience, when becoming weary with examining, we suddenly conclude that we have done enough, and understand the whole subject.

" From prejudice, in two ways exteriorly or judging from appearances, and interiorly : exteriorly, when we trust too easily to the report of others, not reflecting that the reporters may deceive, or are themselves deceived ; interiorly, when we are inclined to believe one thing in preference to another without good reasons.

" The greatest irregularity of the mind is, to believe things because we wish them to be true, and not because we have actually discovered that they are so. Our passions draw us into this fault, for we are disposed to believe what we wish for, whether it be true or not. Frequently when we dread an occurrence, we are unwilling to believe that it has happened, and often, through weakness, we believe that it will occur. An angry person always thinks his cause just, without even being willing to consent to examine circumstances, therefore he is incapable of judging.

" This seduction of the passions has a momentous influence over our lives, both on account of the objects that incessantly present themselves, and our native humor which impels us almost irresistibly to certain particular inclinations, which we would discover predominant in us, if we knew better how to observe our own character and conduct. And as we always desire to bend our reason to our wishes, we call *right* whatever is the most conformable to our natural humor, that is, to a secret passion, which is so much the more obvious as it forms the groundwork of our nature.

" Hence we have said, that the greatest evil arising from the passions, is, that they prevent us from reasoning well, and consequently from judging accurately, for sound judgment is the result of sound reasoning.

" It is also obvious from what has been advanced, that sloth which dreads the trouble of examining thoroughly is one of the greatest obstacles to judging well. This defect is allied to impatience, for indolence ever impatient, when exertion is required, inclines us *to believe* rather than to *examine*, for the first is easily performed, while the latter requires long and tedious research. Good advice always appears too prolix to the slothful person ; so he relinquishes all effort, and accustoms himself to be led by any one that will guide him like a child or blind man.

" The mind is so captivated and seduced by all the causes mentioned, that it thinks it knows what it does not know, and that it judges justly when it is deceived. Not that it does not clearly distinguish the difference between knowing and not knowing, or being deceived; for it is well aware that one is not the other, and even that no two things can be more opposite; but from want of reflection, it wishes to believe that it knows what it does not know.

"Our ignorance is so profound, that most frequently we do not know our own dispositions. A man is unwilling to believe that he is proud, ungenerous, indolent, or passionate. He wishes to think himself upright, and, though his conscience often reproaches him with his faults, he prefers smothering these thoughts to entertaining the disagreeable emotions that accompany the knowledge of them.

"The vice which hinders us from knowing our defects is denominated self-love, and it is this that leads us to give so much credit to the flatterer.

"It is impossible to overcome the numerous obstacles which hinder us from judging accurately, or from discovering *truth*, unless we entertain a great love for it, and have an ardent desire to understand it.

"From this it is apparent that judging falsely frequently springs from a defect in the will. The understanding was formed for judging, and whenever it *comprehends fully* it judges accurately. Therefore, if it deduces wrong conclusions, it is not sufficiently informed; and not to be well informed concerning a subject on which we are required to judge, is really comprehending nothing to the purpose, for the judgment must be derived from the entire subject.

"Consequently, whatever we understand is true. When we are deceivēd, it is because we do not understand, and the false is in reality naught; therefore, neither comprehensible nor intelligible. The true exists, the false exists not.

"We may fail in comprehending what exists; but we can never understand what has no existence. Persons sometimes imagine they understand a nonentity, and this produces error; but, in reality, they do not understand it; for it is not. The reason why we think we understand what we do not *comprehend*, is, for the same reasons, or rather weaknesses, that we have mentioned. Persons will not reflect, however they wish to judge, and they judge precipitately; and, in fine, they wish to think that they have understood fully, and hence they deceive themselves.

"No man willfully deceives himself, and so no man would be deceived if he did not will the things that cause him to be deceived: because he wishes those things which hinder him from meditating, and seriously endeavoring to find the truth.

"So he who is deceived, first, does not understand his object; and, second, does not understand himself, because he will not consider his object nor himself, nor precipitation, impatience, and sloth, with those passions and prejudices which cause this deception.

"And it rema'ns certain that the understanding, purified of its vices and really attentive to its object, will never be deceived, because it will then either see clearly, and what it perceives will be certain, or it will not see clearly, and it will hold it certain that it ought to doubt until the light appears."

We have considered it useful to extract this lengthy quotation from Bossuet's "De la Connaissance de Dieu et de soi-même," because the cause of our errors is of the utmost importance in Logic, and should form the daily subject of the meditation and reflection of pupils; and we can not too earnestly recommend young ladies to learn how to define clearly, to determine distinctly, and to avoid carefully all the causes of error.

CHAPTER II.

OF PROPOSITIONS.

Question. What is a Proposition?

Answer. It is the expression of a judgment.

Q. Of how many parts must a proposition consist?

A. Of three parts; which are, the subject, the verb, and the predicate.

As we have already explained each of these three parts, we will now treat of the properties of propositions, and of their different species.

ARTICLE FIRST.

OF THE PROPERTIES OF PROPOSITIONS.

Among propositions we distinguish absolute propositions, and relative propositions.

Question. What is an absolute proposition?

Answer. An absolute proposition is one that is independent of every other proposition; it expresses the principal subject of thought, and contains within itself complete sense.

Q. What is a relative proposition ?

A. It is one that depends upon another proposition, with which it is so intimately connected that we can not omit it, or retrench any part of it, without subtracting an idea necessarily connected with the first idea, and expressed in the principal absolute proposition.

OF THE ABSOLUTE PROPERTIES OF PROPOSITIONS.

Question. What are the absolute properties of propositions?

Answer. The absolute properties of propositions are quantity and quality.

Q. What is the quantity of a proposition ?

A. It is the extension of its subject, or the development of its kind. By this extension we discover whether the proposition is universal, particular, singular, or indefinite.

Q. What is a universal proposition ?

A. A universal proposition is one whose subject comprehends an entire genus or species, as *all*, any *one*, *each one*. Such are the following propositions : " *Every body is divisible;*" " *No spirit is mortal ;*" " *Each one thinks of his own interests.*"

Q. What is a particular proposition ?

A. A particular proposition denotes a limited

4*

or partial *meaning* of the subject, or signifies that it does not include an entire genus or species; and in this case the restricting words, *some, few, many,* &c., usually *precede* the subject of the proposition. Such are the following propositions: "*A certain man is the author of this book;*" "*Few men spend their time to the best advantage;*" "*Many persons repent of folly when too late.*"

Q. What is a singular proposition?

A. A singular proposition has one individual for its subject; as, "*Alexander conquered the Persians;*" "*Cæsar was assassinated in the Senate house.*"

Q. What is an indefinite proposiiton?

A. An indefinite proposition relates to *one* individual, among *many of the same nature*, without, however, including universality, particularity, or singularity; as, "*A circle is a figure, an angle is a figure;*" "*A wise man conducts his affairs with discretion.*"

General Rule.—Every proposition must either be allied to universality or to particularity, for, in every proposition, the subject is either taken according to its whole extent, or to a part of its extent; if the subject be taken in its full extent, the proposition is universal; in the contrary case, it is particular.

OF THE QUALITY OF PROPOSITIONS.

A proposition is either affirmative or negative, true or false.

Question. What is an affirmative proposition?

Answer. It is one whose subject is joined to its predicate.

Q. What is a negative proposition?

A. It is one in which the predicate is denied to the subject by means of a negation.

Q. When is a proposition true?

A. A true proposition is one that expresses its subject as it really is, or conformable to ideas; as, " *God is supremely good.*"

Q. When is a proposition false?

A. When it represents its subject in a manner contrary to ideas, and otherwise than it is; as, " *God is cruel.*"

Every logical proposition is either true or false. If it presents its object such as it is, the proposition is true; if, on the contrary, it presents it with characters that are foreign to it, the proposition is false.

Q. How can we judge of the truth of a proposition?

A. To judge of the truth of a proposition, we

must form exact ideas of the subject and predicate, and compare them. If, in comparing them, we discover that the idea of the predicate is comprised in all that bears the name of subject, the proposition will be admitted universally true; if, on the contrary, this predicate agrees with some subjects and is not found in others, it will be reckoned among the number of particular ones; therefore it is necessary to know upon what a proposition hinges before deciding upon its universality.

Q. How do you discern that a proposition is false?

A. When, after comparing the predicate with the subject, I find that the predicate does not at all agree with the subject.

Q. Are there not propositions that are both true and false?

A. Every proposition is either true or false. It is true if the declaration it expresses is such as it expresses it. In the opposite case it is false. But to show to what an extent the subtlety of sophistry has been carried, we borrow from a logician the responses to some objections, celebrated in the schools.

For example: If Peter says, "*I lie*," without having previously spoken, this proposition is at the same time true and false; for if it be true it is likewise false, because while saying "*I lie*," Peter tells the truth, therefore he did not tell a lie; and if it be true that he lies when he says, "*I lie*," then he tells the truth. This proposition is therefore true and false at the same time ; or rather it is neither true nor false.

So, also, if the guardian of a bridge had received orders to throw into the river all those who do not tell the truth, and Peter were to say to him: "You must throw *me* into the river." If Peter has told the truth he must not be thrown into the river ; but if Peter is not thrown into the river, he will have told the keeper a falsehood, and he must be thrown into the river : therefore this is a sort of proposition in which its truth must result from its falsity, and vice versa. Therefore, every proposition is not either true or false.

I reply to the first objection :—

The first proposition is purely grammatical, because it is expressed as propositions in grammar are ; but it is not logical, because it expresses no judgment; for, how can he lie, who has not previously spoken? It would be necessary that Peter should have spoken beforehand, and then the proposition would refer to what Peter had said. Now, we have here no question of propositions but such as are logical, and therefore expressive of judgments.

As to the second objection, it may be said that the keeper of the bridge has received an order to throw into the river, not those who would say: "You must throw me into the river;" but those who told a falsehood which had reference to something else—something incomplete—*and to do so*, in punishment of the falsehood.

We have dwelt upon these contradictory propositions, in order to demonstrate their puerility; for it only too frequently happens that persons consider themselves witty in putting forth such propositions; but they only serve to falsify the judgment.

Q. Can a proposition have several meanings?

A. It may be natural, that is, employed in its proper sense; it may also be employed in a sense that is foreign to it.

Q. What is the proper sense of a proposition?

A. A proposition is employed in its proper or appropriate sense, when all the words that compose it preserve their natural signification; if otherwise, it would be employed in a sense foreign to it.

The natural and proper meaning of a proposition is also divided into its literal sense and its metaphorical sense.

In the literal sense, every word that constitutes the proposition preserves its proper sense; on the contrary, in the metaphorical sense, this proper signification is transferred to a foreign signification in virtue of a comparison, as when I say, when speaking of a powerful and courageous man, "*He is a lion.*"

The meaning of a proposition is again separated into a compound and divided sense.

Q. What is the compound sense of a proposition?

A. Propositions that have a compound meaning are divided into four classes: 1. Exclusives; 2. Comparatives; 3. Exceptives; 4. Inceptives or Desitives.

OF EXCLUSIVES.

Exclusive propositions are those which denote that a predicate agrees with a subject, and that it agrees with that subject alone. Hence, they include two different judgments, and, consequently, they are compound in their meaning. Example: "*God alone is to be loved solely for Himself.*" It is as if we said: "*We ought to love God for Himself, and love other things only for God.*" "Pious men are the sole favorites of Heaven."

OF COMPARATIVES.

A comparative proposition also includes two judgments; because first we declare a thing is so, and then we repeat that it is so, in a greater or less degree than another; as, "*Better are the wounds of a friend than the deceitful kisses of an enemy;*" "*The heaviest loss is that of a faithful friend.*"

OF EXCEPTIVES.

We call exceptives, those propositions in which we affirm a thing of a whole subject, except some subordinates of that subject, proving by some exceptive particularity, that what is predicated of the subject does not agree with those subordinates. This obviously comprises two judgments, and thus renders this kind of proposition compound in meaning, as when I say:—

None of the sects among the ancient philosophers, except the Platonists, admitted that God was incorporeal. This means: 1. That the ancient philosophers believed God to be corporeal; and 2. That the Platonists believed the reverse.

The following propositions are also exceptives:

The miser does nothing good, except to die.

No one thinks himself unhappy, except while comparing himself with those who are happier.

We have no ills but those we create for our selves.

Observe that the exclusive and the exceptive propositions are nearly the same thing expressed somewhat differently, so that it is always quite easy to exchange them reciprocally.

OF INCEPTIVES OR DESITIVES.

When we say that a thing has begun to be such, or that it has ceased to be such, we form two judgments; one concerning what that thing was previous to the time of which we are speaking; the other, of what it is since; and thus, such propositions, some of which are called inceptive, and others desitive, are compound in sense, and they are so nearly alike, that it appears to us more accurate to reduce them to one species, and treat them together.

Example: The Jews began, after the return from Babylon, to omit using their ancient letters, which are those that are now called Samaritan.

The Latin language has ceased to be the vulgar tongue in' Italy for nearly 700 years.

The Jews only began, in the fifth century of the Christian era, to use points to designate their vowels.

Such propositions contradict each other, according to each reference to the separate epochs. Thus, some deny the last, pretending, though falsely, that the Jews have always used points, at least for reading vowels, and that the points were kept in the Temple; and others assert that the use of points is even posterior to the fifth century.

We will not dwell longer upon contradictory propositions, for common sense is all that is requisite for refuting the defective reasoning on which they are founded.

The conversion of propositions, or the changing of the subject into the place of the predicate, and still retaining the quality of the propositions, appearing to be of no great utility, we omit the principles of it, so as to explain the remaining propositions.

ARTICLE SECOND.

OF THE DIFFERENT SORTS OF PROPOSITIONS.

It has already been said that the proposition in respect to its *quantity*, is divided into universal, particular, and infinite. In respect to its *quality*, it is divided into affirmative and negative. It remains to speak of its form, its subject, and its division.

Question. How many propositions are there in respect to form?

Answer. Two—absolute and incidental.

Q. How many kinds in respect to matter?

A. The proposition is simple or compound, complex or incomplex.

Q. When is a proposition simple, and when complex?

A. A proposition is simple when it represents but one subject and one predicate, without adding a complement to one or the other.

A proposition, on the contrary, is complex when it adds a complement to either the subject or predicate, or to both: as, " The Lord Almighty created this fleeting world." Almighty is the complement of the subject, fleeting is the complement of the predicate.

But if I said: " The Lord Almighty created this world, which is destined to be destroyed," not only those words, " which is destined to be destroyed," would form the complement of the predicate, but they would further constitute a second proposition, which is called incidental.

Q. What is an incidental proposition?

A. It is one that is brought in to complete the sense of another proposition.

Q. How many sorts of incidental propositions are there?

A. Two; incidental determinative, and incidental explicative.

Q. What is the incidental determinative?

A. It is one that is so joined to the principal proposition, and so necessary to it, that it can not be retrenched without injuring the sense of the phrase, as this: "*All men who have led holy lives will be saved.*" If I retrench the proposition "*who have led holy lives,*" it is clear that I state a false proposition, because there would remain the proposition: "*All men will be saved.*" Hence the proposition, *who have led holy lives*, is absolutely necessary to the meaning of my phrase; therefore, it is an incidental determinative.

Q. What is the proposition explicative?

A. It is a proposition added to another proposition to render it more clear, but as it is not essential to the formation of the phrase, it may be retrenched without injuring its sense; for instance: if I say, "Men, who are mortal, should always be prepared for death." The words, "*who are mortal,*" being a simple explanation, may easily be retrenched without injuring the meaning of the phrase.

Q. What is a compound proposition?

A. A compound proposition is one whose subject or predicate is multiple, that is, not formed of one sole object or one sole predicate, as is the simple proposition. Example: " The Loire, the Seine, and the Rhone, water France." It is evident that this proposition is compound, for it is as if I said, the Loire waters France, the Seine waters France, the Rhone waters France. But as I denote but one single action done at once, though by three different subjects, I need but one proposition, which I denominate compound.

Students in grammar are requested to pay attention to this principle, for many reckon in phrases of this kind as many propositions as there are subjects. True, there are grammatically as many propositions in a phrase, as there are finite verbs, that is, as there are different actions performed by different subjects. But if the subjects express but one action done at the same time by all the subjects, there will be only one proposition, which we shall call compound.

The various propositions considered in reference to their use, serve for a great number of things. Sometimes the proposition is employed to explain the nature of a thing ; it is then called a definition. Examples : Kingdoms are but an atom of dust, the world only a tent which is set up to-day and removed to morrow. Tyranny is an unlimited monarchy. Magnanimity is a benevolence which aims at behaving nobly. Melancholy is at the same time pain and pleasure; pain in the regret, pleasure in the remembrance.

Sometimes the proposition serves to divide a whole into its parts, it is then called *division*. Sometimes it expresses a truth so obvious that it can not be doubted, it is then called *an axiom ;* or it contains some general truth whence several other particular truths are deduced, and then it is termed *a principle*. Sometimes it serves to demonstrate other propositions, under the name of *lemma ;* or it expresses the property of some object by demonstration, as : "*A triangle is equal to two right angles ;* in this case it is a *theorem ;* or it expresses some operation to be performed concerning an object, as : " A triangle being given, what space will two triangles fill similar in all respects to the first ?" and this is called a *problem*. When a proposition is obviously deduced from a demonstrated proposition, it is a *corollary*. When it serves to illustrate an explanation already given, so as to leave no doubt or obscurity, it is called a *scholium*.

Q. Among all the propositions that have been enumerated, which are the chief and most frequently used ?

A. The principal propositions are the Definition and the Division.

OF THE DEFINITION.

Question. What is the definition?

Answer. Definition is a discourse that tends to explain whatever is obscure or not distinctly understood in the first expression.

Q. How many kinds of definition are there?

A. Two; definition of names, and definition of things.

Q. What is the definition of a name?

A. It is explaining what we mean by that name.

Q. What is the definition of a thing?

A. It is the explaining what is the nature of that thing; for instance: when I say, "Man is an animal that reasons," I tell the nature of man; 1st, by making known what he possesses in common with other beings; and 2d, by making known in what he differs from other beings.

A. What word do you use to express what one object has in common with another?

A. The word Genus (plu. Genera). Thus, in the definition given above, the word *animal* is the genus, which is applied to man as well as to beasts, because, like them, he is animate.

Q. By what term do you express that property of an object which serves to distinguish it from other objects?

A. The word Difference. Thus, in that same definition, the word *reasons*, is the difference, because it serves to distinguish man from other animals.

Q. How many kinds of definition has a name?

A. Two; the common and the particular. The common definition of a name is the one that is commonly given to it; the particular definition is one that we use when we aim at merely expressing a thought accurately, without troubling ourselves whether others accept it in the same sense.

Q. How many sorts of definition are there for things?

A. Two; one is the definition properly so called, and which aims only at explaining the nature of an object; and the other which extends to all the qualities and properties of the object. The latter is called *description*. As there are in nature a great number of things that men can not yet define, they content themselves with describing their properties to make them better known. Thus, Physicists can neither define electricity, nor the magnet, because they are not sufficiently acquainted with their nature, although they know a number of their properties.

Q. What properties are requisite for a good definition?

A. There are four; the first is clearness; that is, it makes known the nature of the thing to be defined, and that it contain no obscure term, no ambiguous or double meaning.

The second is conciseness; that is, there must be nothing superfluous, for useless words are injurious to clearness.

The third is reciprocity; that is, the definition should so distinctly represent the thing defined, that we may, while only reading the definition, say with certainty it means such an object.

The fourth is, that it show obviously both the genus and the difference.

OF DIVISION.

Question. What is Division?

Answer. It is the distribution of a whole into its different parts, or of a genus into its different species; the first is called partition, the second division.

Q. What qualities are requisite for a good division?

A. 1. Entireness or completeness, that we may easily recognize the parts; 2. Oppositeness, that

5

is, that some members may not be included in others, because the parts that compose a whole must be distinct.   There should not be any thing interposed between the members of a division, for, the terms of the division should be first clearly expressed, and then we may pass to subdivisions if the subject require it.

If we learn to define well and divide properly we shall have learned how to arrange our thoughts in suitable order, and to express them clearly.   This study is of the highest importance, as discussions almost always spring from mutual misapprehension.

THIRD PART.

Reasoning may be considered in respect to its existence *within* the mind, when it preserves the title Reasoning, but if it be expressed exteriorly it is called Argumentation.

CHAPTER I.

OF REASONING, CONSIDERED IN RESPECT TO ITS EXISTENCE WITHIN THE MIND.

By judging is meant, comparing two ideas, and discovering or perceiving that the second idea is contained in the first. But as it often happens that our ideas of a compound object are not sufficiently exact to assure us that it contains a certain predicate that we compare with it, although this predicate is actually contained in it; in such case, to enable us to pass from doubt to certainty, and say with security: "*I see that the idea of the subject includes the idea of the predicate,* or *excludes the predicate,"* we must extend the predicate, and join to this first idea other ideas that will enable us to distinguish clearly the idea of the predicate.

Therefore, reasoning, is explaining the relation of two ideas by means of a third which inserts the second in the first.

When the ideas that we compare are so clear that we perceive at once their agreement or disagreement, it is useless to have recourse to a third idea; as when we judge of propositions so obvious that they need no proof, and are thence called self-evident propositions, as: "*The whole is greater than any of its parts."* But it is when we can not see at once whether two ideas agree or disagree with each other, that we are obliged to borrow the aid of a third idea wherewith to compare them, and discover whether they are unsuitable to each other. This third idea is called *arugment* or middle term.

Question. Give an illustration, to render the above more clear.

Answer. Every one knows that the earth is a vast solid mass, composed of land and water, containing plants, animals, &c.; but every one does not know that the earth is round. In order to convince a person who would doubt the latter, we must amplify the idea she has already concerning the earth, and lead her to discover its roundness. To attain to it, I could prove to her that the shadow of a round body is always in the form of a perfect cone; and experience proves, from eclipses of the moon, that the earth's shadow always has this shape. Observe, the conical shadow is included in the idea of the earth's shadow. In this idea of the earth, which is amplified by the above remark, we recognize the idea of round bodies, and thus we are led to the idea of the earth, which includes the idea of roundness.

Q. How do you define reasoning?

A. Reasoning is a simple act of the mind, by which we deduce a judgment or conclusion, from several other judgments or conclusions.

CHAPTER II.

In the general view of Argumentation already presented, we spoke of the matter and form of the syllogism. Before proceeding to the general rules of syllogisms we propose giving a few counsels, which appear to us profitable because they may be considered as a foundation on which we may rest when we reason.

1. Avoid puerile questions in which, under the specious title of " jeu d'esprit," or witticism, the judgment becomes depraved.

2. When you are about to enter upon an argument, first settle with accuracy the state of the question. It often happens that persons dispute without comprehending each other because they have not thoroughly laid down the terms of the debate; they pronounce the same words without assigning to them the same ideas, each one upholding her own views and neither having strength sufficient to vanquish the other.

When the question has been clearly stated, beware of forgetting it, and of bringing out proofs which presume it to be other than it is. This leads persons to become excited and even irritated with efforts to prove what is not disputed, and to contest for concessions that have already been granted. Avoid also that inordinate desire of arguing and contradicting, which gives an air of pedantry extremely unbecoming in any one, but particularly in one of the gentle sex, who should never contest seriously except for the advantage of establishing some salutary truth.

It is chiefly in bringing out comparisons to prove what we have advanced that we are most liable to digress from the stated question.

Never deduce general conclusions from particular instances; nay, it is perfectly illogical to do so; it is a great defect into which those fall who are governed by a party spirit. Thus if some abuses have crept into an institution, it is not thence to be considered that the institution is radically evil.

The enemies of religion will say that some ecclesiastics have deviated from the path of duty, and they conclude from it that the whole body of the clergy needs reform. We might answer: Wine is certainly an excellent thing; but how many without any good motive daily abuse the use of this beverage, which thus becomes to them the source of the most lamentable misfortunes. Must we on this account destroy all the vineyards, and proscribe the use of wine?

St. Paul, the Apostle, exhorts us "*not to be carried away with every wind of doctrine.*" Never expose yourself by adopting too readily the principles and views of the first person you hear on any subject, for you would run the risk of being grossly deceived. Listen attentively and examine carefully before surrendering to the opinions advanced. In such circumstances the art of reasoning will prove of great service to you.

Finally, always define clearly the terms that compose the question, and compare them by putting the definition in the place of the object defined. By this precaution you will avoid discussing questions destitute of meaning, and composed of words which, when compared, signify nothing. Certain terms, at first sight, sometimes appear to convey a great deal, but when reduced to their real value, astonish us by their trivialness, and we perceive that the dispute is vain and childish, and based on words alone.

We will conclude these counsels to our young friends by an example of erroneous reasoning, well fitted to prove the necessity of carefully defining terms.

Example: A good man, very enthusiastic in his zeal for religion, might perhaps tell you:—

" Study, meditate, and compare the Sacred Writings, for they contain the only useful science; all other knowledge is vain."

Here we have, without doubt, a good counsel; but the manner of stating it is not perfectly accurate; if we examine the definitions of the words study, meditate, and compare, it will be readily perceived that we can not *meditate*, and *compare*, without first having learned the art of meditation and comparison; therefore there are other kinds of useful knowledge besides that contained in the Sacred Writings; therefore the knowledge of Holy Scripture is not the sole, indispensable science; and it becomes inexact to say that all other kinds of knowledge are useless.

ARTICLE FIRST.

ON THE RULES OF SYLLOGISMS.

The ancients have transmitted to us eight perfectly lucid rules, and these the moderns have reduced to *one* only.

RULE 1.—There can be but three terms in a syllogism, the major, the minor, and middle term; because, the syllogism being constructed to prove

5*

that the extremes agree or disagree, it suffices that we find these three terms in a syllogism. The following syllogism would be defective:—

Every man is a reasoning animal;
Every angel is a spirit:
Therefore, every angel is a reasoning animal.

The reason is, that there are four different terms, viz., man, animal, angel, and spirit.

RULE 2.—The term in the conclusion must never be taken more universally than it is in the premises.

The conclusion is derived from the premises; therefore it is contained in the premises; but what is less universal does not contain what is more universal; therefore, a term should not be more universal in the conclusion than it is in the premises; for this reason the following syllogism is defective:—

Every body is a substance;
No spirit is corporeal:
. Therefore, no spirit is a substance.

For in the major, the word substance is taken particularly as the predicate of the affirmative proposition; and it is taken universally in the conclusion as the predicate of the negative proposition.

RULE 3.—The middle term must not appear in the conclusion. The conclusion is a proposition which expresses only the agreement disagreement of the two extremes; such a proposition can not contain the middle term, for the proposition which expresses the agreement or disagreement of the two extremes, ought not to contain the reason why these two extremes agree or disagree; but, the middle term is that reason for which the two extremes agree or disagree; therefore, it must not be contained in the conclusion.

Hence the following syllogism is defective:—

Peter is little;

Peter is a philosopher:

Therefore, Peter is a little philosopher;

For Peter which is the middle term is found anew in the conclusion.

RULE 4.—The middle term must be taken universally once, at least, in the premises.

According to the first rule, a syllogism should contain only three terms; if the middle term be not taken universally in the premises, there will be four terms in the syllogism, thus, it would become double, and would signify two different things; if the middle term be employed twice in the premises, it would signify two different things, for the part of its extension employed in one of the premises, would not be the same as the part of the extension employed in the other premises; therefore, &c.

Hence the following syllogism is faulty :—

Every man is an animal ;

Every beast is an animal :

Therefore, every beast is a man.

The word animal, the middle term, is taken particularly in both affirmative premises of which it is the predicate, and signifies two different things.

RULE 5.—From two negative premises nothing can be concluded. For they separate the middle term from the two extremes (or the subject and predicate of the conclusion), and when two ideas disagree with a third, we can not infer that they either agree or disagree with each other ; thus, that two staves are not equal to a third staff, does not lead us to conclude that they are equal to each other. The following syllogism is therefore faulty :—

Man is not made of stone ;

Marble is not a man :

Therefore, marble is not a stone.

Remark. A proposition may be affirmative in the syllogism, and negative out of the syllogism. Thus in the following syllogism :—

He who does not honor God, will not be saved ;

The impious man does not honor God :

Therefore, the impious man will not be saved.

" *He who honors not God* " is the middle term, and the subject of the second proposition, so that the minor (which out of the syllogism would be negative) is affirmative in this syllogism; for the minor is equivalent to, " *The impious man is the man who does not honor God.* " But out of the syllogism, this proposition is equivalent to, " *The impious man does not honor God,* " which is negative.   This proposition is therefore really not the same out of the syllogism and in the syllogism, but is merely so in appearance, and the syllogism quoted above has not two negative premises.   But why has not the second proposition the same meaning in and out of the syllogism ?   It is because the major modifies the sense of the minor; but out of the syllogism there is nothing to change the sense.

RULE 6.—Two affirmative premises can never produce a negative conclusion.

When two premises are affirmative, the two extremes which are found in the premises, agree with the middle term; but because the two extremes agree with the middle term, we can not conclude that they disagree with each other: it is the reverse; the conclusion must therefore be affirmative, according to the following principle: two things which are equal to a third, are equal to each other; therefore, &c.

Hence the following syllogism is faulty:—
Every good thing is lovely;
Virtue is a good thing:
Therefore, virtue is not love.

RULE 7.—From two particular premises nothing can be deduced. Two particular premises are either both affirmative, or both negative, or again, one is affirmative and the other negative, and in any case no conclusion can be deduced.

1. If they are negative, we can conclude nothing, as has been demonstrated by Rule 5th. 2. If they are particular affirmatives, nothing can be concluded, because in that case the middle term would be taken twice particularly, which is forbidden by Rule 4th. 3. We can conclude nothing if one is affirmative and the other negative ; for in this hypothesis the conclusion would become negative, as we shall see in Rule 8th. The great extreme would be taken universally in the conclusion as predicate of the negative proposition; it would then be necessary to take it universally in the premises, according to Rule 2d.

Then, there would have to be two terms taken universally in the premises, viz.: the great extreme, according to Rule 2d, and the middle term according to Rule 4th; but two terms could not be taken universally in particular premises, one of which is affirmative and the other

negative; for the premises are composed of four
terms, the double subject and the double predicate.   Of these four terms, three are taken particularly, in the particular premises, of which one
is affirmative, and the other negative, namely:
the two subjects of the particular propositions,
and the predicate of the affirmative proposition.

Therefore, from two particular premises, one
being affirmative and the other negative, nothing
can be legitimately deduced.   Thus, because a
man is a physician and a man is poor, we can not
conclude that physicians are either rich or poor.

RULE 8.—The conclusion always follows the
weaker part.   That is to say:—1. If one of the
premises be negative, the conclusion must be
negative.   For if the middle term be denied of
either part of the conclusion, it may show that
the terms of the conclusion disagree, but it can
never show that they agree.   Hence, the following syllogism is faulty:—

No animal is a plant;
Every ox is an animal:
Therefore, every ox is a plant.

To render this syllogism good, conclude thus:—

Therefore, no ox is a plant.

2. If either of the premises be particular, the
conclusion must be particular, or the conclusion
can not be universal.

For, if this be not so, we must affirm or deny,
of *every* subject in the conclusion, what has been
only affirmed or denied of one subject in the
premises, and, consequently, take one term in
the conclusion more universally than we took it
in the premises, which is forbidden by the fourth
rule. Therefore, if one of the premises is particular, the conclusion must, of necessity, be so
also.

The defect of the following syllogism will be
easily discerned, in which the conclusion is a
universal affirmative, although one of the premises is particular:—

Every body has extension;
Some substances are bodies:
Therefore, every substance has extension.

RULES OF SYLLOGISMS ACCORDING TO THE MOD-
ERNS.

The moderns admit only one general rule,
which contains all the others, and may be substituted for them; it is this:—

*One of the premises must contain the conclu-
sion, and the other, declare that it is therein contained.*

In negative syllogisms, the negative premise
always contains the conclusion, and the affirma-

tive premise declares that the conclusion is contained in the negative premise. But in affirmative syllogisms, either of the premises may contain the conclusion, or may declare that it is contained in the other premise.

The following syllogism will render this rule more clear:—

Every virtue is laudable;

Temperance is a virtue:

Therefore, temperance is laudable.

In this syllogism, the great extreme, or the predicate of the conclusion "laudable," is contained in the major.

The lesser extreme, or the subject of the conclusion, is also included in the major, temperance; for the minor declares that temperance is a virtue, therefore it is included in the words, " every virtue."

ARTICLE SECOND.

OF THE DIFFERENT KINDS OF SYLLOGISMS.

Question. Name the principal kinds of syllogisms.

Answer. They may be reduced to three: the simple, the complex, and the compound. The simple syllogism is the one of which we have hitherto spoken; the complex is one whose conclusion is a complex proposition; as the following :—

The divine law ordains that princes be honored;

Louis is a prince:

Therefore, the divine law ordains that Louis be honored.

Q. How can we ascertain whether a complex syllogism is correct?

A. By reducing it to a simple syllogism, and then examining whether it contains all the conditions required for the simple syllogism.

Q. What is a compound syllogism?

A. It is one in which the major is compound.

Q. How do you divide the compound syllogism?

A. Into three kinds: the conditional, the copulative, and the disjunctive.

Q. What is a conditional syllogism?

A. It is one whose major is conditional.

If God is just, He will punish sinners;

God is just:

Therefore, He punishes sinners.

Again :—

Q. What is a disjunctive syllogism?

A. It is one in which the major is disjunctive. This syllogism may be reduced to the conditional.

Example:

The earth moves either in a circle, or in an ellipse;

But it does not move in a circle;

Therefore, it moves in an ellipse.

The action of Brutus in killing Cæsar was either an act of virtue, or a crime;

It was not an act of virtue;

Therefore, it was a crime.

It is by reducing the disjunctive syllogism to the conditional, that we perceive the absurdity of a great number of sophisms, as the following:—

Either you are learned, or not learned;

You are not learned;

Therefore, you are learned.

Changed into a conditional, this syllogism is reduced to the following words, which are destitute of meaning:—

You are learned, if you are not learned.

The first conditional proposition is sufficient to prove to us how destitute it is of sense.

Q. What is the copulative syllogism?

A. It is one in which the major is copulative.

Example:—

No one can serve God and Mammon;

The covetous man serves Mammon;

Therefore, he does not serve God.

Or the minor may run thus:—

The true Christian serves God;
Therefore, he does not serve Mammon.

NOTE.—Reasoning by syllogisms is only used
in philosophy. The philosopher who aims at
discovering truth always dreads mistakes, so he
advances syllogism in hand, as the geometrician
with his compass. The orator can not confine
himself to the dryness and stiffness of philosophical argumentation. Thus, instead of saying,
like a logician,
All men are mortal;
You are a man :
Therefore you are mortal.

The author and orator supress the major, and
simply say : Thou art man, and consequently
mortal.

ARTICLE THIRD.

OF DIFFERENT KINDS OF REASONING, BESIDES THE SYLLOGISM.

Question. In addition to the Syllogism, how
many kinds of reasoning are there ?

Answer. Six: the Prosyllogism, the Enthymeme, the Epichirema, the Sorites, the Dilemma, and the Induction.

Q. What is a Prosyllogism?

A. It is a mode of reasoning formed of five propositions, that contain two syllogisms so connected that the conclusion of the former is the major or minor of the following. Example:

Things that have no composition of parts are indissoluble;

A spiritual substance has no composition of parts;

Therefore, a spiritual substance is indissoluble:

Now the human mind is a spiritual substance;

Therefore, the human mind is indissoluble.

Q. What is an Enthymeme?

A. An argument consisting of only two propositions, an antecedent, and a consequent derived from it; as " *We are dependent, therefore we should be humble.*" Here the major proposition is suppressed. The complete syllogism would be :—

Dependent creatures should be humble;

We are dependent creatures:

Therefore we should be humble.

Scholium. In enthymemes there is a particular elegance, especially when they are used in common conversation, because, as they do not display an argument in all its parts, they offer to the exercise and invention of the mind that scope which they delight to take. In fine writing, it is a great secret so to frame and put together our thoughts as to give full play to the reader's imagination, and draw him insensibly into our views and course of reasoning.

Q. What is the Epichirema?

A. A sort of syllogism in which each of the premises is accompanied by its proof.—(A prolix kind of argument.) Example: He who is agitated by a multitude of cares is not happy; for tranquillity of mind is the principal requisite for happiness. Now the man who abandons himself to his passions, is agitated by a multitude of cares, either on account of remorse of conscience which incessantly torments him, or because he can not always satisfy his desires; therefore he who abandons himself to his passions is not happy.

This kind of reasoning is advantageous as it leaves no doubt in the mind.

Q. What is the Sorites?

A. An abridged form of stating a series of syllogisms, in which the conclusion of each is a premise to the succeeding one.

Example:

There can be no enjoyment of property without government;

No government without laws enforced;

No laws enforced without a magistrate;

No magistrate without obedience;

No obedience; where every one acts as he pleases:

Therefore there can be no enjoyment of prop erty where every one acts as he pleases.

A Sorites may be formed of Hypothetical Enthymenes, any number of which may be so joined in a series that the consequent of each shall become the antecedent of the next following; in which case, by establishing the antecedent of the first we establish the consequent of the last ; or, by removing the consequent of the last we remove the antecedent of the first. Example:

If men are to be punished in another world, God must be the punisher ;

If God be the punisher, the punishment must be just ;

If the punishment be just, the punished must be guilty ;

If the punished be guilty, they could have done otherwise ;

If they could have done otherwise, they were free agents :

Therefore if men are liable to punishment in another world they must be free.*

When one idea alone is not sufficient to demonstrate clearly the relation of the conclusion of two extremes, the sorites is employed ; but the sorites will be defective, if all the particular

propositions are not well linked, so that the conclusion follows from each last link ; as :

He who drinks well, sleeps well ;

He who sleeps well, does not sin ;

He who does not sin, will be saved :

Therefore, he who drinks well, will be saved.

The falsity of the above sorites is so evident
that it needs no explanation.

Plutarch relates that the Thracians, finding a
frozen river in their passage, let loose a fox before them to find out whether they might pass
over the ice in security : the fox puts his ear
close to the ice, and hearing the murmuring of
the water, stops short, and appears to reason
interiorly thus :

Whatever makes a noise moves ;

Whatever moves is not frozen ;

What is not frozen is liquid ;

Liquid yields to the pressure of weight :

Therefore, the ice is not thick enough to bear me.

Q. What is a Dilemma ?

A. An argument which presents an antagonist
with two or more alternatives, but is equally
conclusive against him whichever alternative he
selects.

A dilemma effected the conversion of Henry
IV. of France ! That prince was a Protestant.
He inquired of the pastors of the Reformed

Church, if people could be saved in that church; they were very careful to inform him that they could be. The king next asked if people could be saved in the Catholic Church, and the pastors replied affirmatively. Then Henry turned to the Catholic prelates and asked them if one could be saved by the Protestant religion: the prelates readily proved to him that it was *impossible*, as it does not bear the marks of the Church presented in the Nicene Creed, viz., Unity, Sanctity, Catholicity, and Apostolicity.

Thereupon the prince constructed a dilemma, which we leave the pupils to arrange as an exercise.

2. Either the souls of the wicked perish at death or they are immortal; if they perish they can have no hope of heaven; if they are immortal they can not hope, but must be continually in dread of judgment: therefore, the wicked can not have any hope of felicity.

3. A sentinel had allowed a camp to be surprised; the general said to him: You were at the post assigned, or you were not; if you were there, you have betrayed the army; if you were not, you have infringed military discipline: therefore you deserve death.

Q. What is Induction?

A. It is a kind of reasoning by which we de-

duce a universal conclusion from several particular conclusions. Thus, if I wish to declare that
all philosophy is useful, I will say :—

Logic is useful;
Natural Philosophy is useful;
Metaphysics are useful;
Mathematics are useful;
Moral science is useful:
Therefore, all Philosophy is useful.

In order that the induction be good, the
enumeration of the parts must be exact, and
none of the parts omitted. The following induction is false, because several parts of the
whole number are left out :—

The French are white; The Germans are
white; The Spanish are white; The English are
white: Hence all men are white.

Because all the nations we have mentioned
are white, it does not follow that the Africans
and the North American Indians are white;
therefore the induction is false.

ARTICLE FOURTH.

OF SOPHISMS.

Question. What is a Sophism ?
Answer. A Sophism is an argument which

contains a latent fallacy under the general appearance of correctness.

We may distinguish two sorts of sophisms, one springs from the understanding, and one from the will.

It frequently happens when disputing, that we forget the conditions or statement of the question, or that the mind has not paid a close attention to the chain of reasoning, or that ignorance hinders us from pursuing the argument to its proper conclusion; each of these defects is a source of sophisms.

When a conclusion is founded upon propositions that are evidently false, the argument that contains them is termed false reasoning; but the title sophism or paralogism is reserved for those arguments that contain principles that *appear* to be true, but which are not so, either because they are not so in the full extent of their meaning, or because they are not accurately arranged for deducing an exact conclusion.

Sometimes common sense shows persons that an argument is sophistic, but they do not possess enough skill to resolve it, and unveil its equivocations. Hence they are not moved by this kind of reasoning, although they do not know how to answer it. We find an example of this in the strange subtleties of the Stoics, as for instance, when they declared, that to live one day, or to live several centuries was one and the same thing.

Virtue is the supreme good.

We can add naught to the supreme good;

For it would not be supreme, if it could be increased. So if a man were happy during one half hour he must have attained supreme felicity, for there is naught beyond it, and ten thousand years of existence could not render him happier.

When, during a discourse based on principles apparently true, an auditor is conducted from consequence to consequence until he arrives at a conclusion that he perceives is palpably false or absurd, he does not consent to it, even though he knows not how to develop the sophism, or prove in what respect it is captious. Such arguments resemble sleight-of-hand tricks, in which the performer appears to do what he does not: the audience seems to perceive the deeds, but no one believes what he sees. Each one is persuaded that the actors are imposing upon him, although he can not explain by what artifice. Therefore, a few features of probability will never be capable of dazzling us so strongly as to lead us to believe absurdities, at least if we are sincerely in search of truth. In vain does a smooth and beautiful path lead to a precipice; far from proceeding to the precipice because the road is inviting, we promptly withdraw from it because of its termination.

When a principle pursued leads on to a manifest absurdity we should renew our investigation of the principle and of every link in the chain of argument. But nothing is more rare than such revisions; it is not pleasant to retrace our steps; a cherished principle joined to labor in which one has fancied that he has succeeded, provokes him to digest the hardest conclusions; and thus blinded he does not perceive the extravagance of his ideas.

We must observe that there is a wide difference between seeing an obvious absurdity in a consequence, absurdity which would force us to revoke a principle of which it is a necessary result, and not being able to answer all the questions and explain all the conclusions to which a principle may give rise; as in the following:—

God has created nothing useless;
Such a plant is useless:
Therefore God did not make it.

How do you know the plant is useless? Because you are ignorant of its properties, must you conclude that it has none? Pray, do men know all things?—is there no knowledge left for them to acquire?

So we frequently hear false principles and sophistical arguments proposed as invincible. If it ever happen to you to hear the shallow reasonings of certain brainless youth against our holy religion, you will promptly recognize the falsity of their principles, for even they themselves, had they a little good-will, would readily perceive it.

Men adopt erroneous principles either because their minds are incapable of reasoning, or because they are not willing to take the trouble of reasoning correctly. They are also, in many cases, influenced by motives of interest. Yet these false principles thus easily adopted falsify our judgment and sometimes withdraw us forever from the practice of virtue.

Worldly minded youth often dispute the maxims of Christianity because they are a reproach to their daily life, but let them examine their principles and they will be forced to change their belief; in changing their creed they must necessarily reform their conduct; and when their conduct is upright they will admit that a little philosophy alienates the mind from religion, but a great deal brings it to her feet.

If the illusions of the senses deceive us by causing us to judge falsely the objects which we see, we must also remember that the passions have a still greater influence over our judgments.

Thus vanity leads us to contemn the views and opinions of others, and to defend our own with warmth.

Friendship inclines us to adopt, without examination, the sentiments of the person whom we like.

The prejudices of youth prompt us to consider the opinions of our parents and instructors as incontestable verities.

. The authority of a person of reputation influences us to such a degree that we trust him on his word alone.

Finally we often venture to pronounce judgments concerning things with which we are but imperfectly acquainted.

Q. Mention some rules, by which we may easily avoid sophisms or paralogisms.

A. It is evident : 1. That if one of the premises is false the conclusion is null.

2. Avoid equivocal terms. An equivocal term is equal to two terms, because we may give it two different meanings, and in that case the syllogism would be considered as having *four* terms.

3. Beware of wandering from the question, and never stop to prove what has not been denied, and never attribute to adversaries opinions which they do not hold.

4. Do not assume the point in question to be true; for in that case there would be no necessity of proving it. This species of sophism is termed *Petitio Principii*, or Begging the Question. The "*Vicious Circle*" may also be considered as belonging to this sort of sophism; it onsists in proving the antecedent by the consequent, and reciprocally the consequent by the antecedent: as if one would wish to prove that the stars twinkle because they are remote from the earth, and reciprocally that they are remote because they twinkle.

5. It is a sophism to assign to an effect any other than its true cause; as, to consider the apparition of a comet the cause of an approaching war: to believe with judicial astrologers that the planets influence the events of life; with a variety of other follies which have led to the saying, that, "Astrology is to astronomy, what superstition is to religion: the silly daughter of a wise mother."

6. The imperfect enumeration of parts must also be ranked among sophisms; thus if we had observed that a hundred inhabitants of a certain town are very honest people, are we authorized to conclude that the whole population is honest?

We may remark that the greater number of

geographers, and notably of travelers, fall into this sophism; for without taking much care to examine, and concluding from particulars to generals they hastily describe manners, customs, and national character. Their conclusions are as absurd as would be that of an itinerant, who when passing through a city, and having been served a capital dinner would inscribe in his note-book: *In this city the people live well, the viands are excellent and well dressed, indeed everybody fares daintily.*

7. It is a sophism to attribute absolutely and without restriction to a thing what belongs to it only by accident. It would be wrong, for instance, to declare that Philosophy is a dangerous science, because some persons make a bad use of it.

8. Avoid the fallacy of division or composition; this fallacy is that where the middle term is used in one premise collectively and in the other distributively. If the middle term is used collectively in the major and distributively in the minor premise, it is the fallacy of division. Example: Christ has said, "It is impossible for a rich man to enter the Kingdom of Heaven." Crœsus is a rich man. Therefore Crœsus can not enter the Kingdom of Heaven. Here the middle term "rich man" is used collectively in the major as meaning all rich men without ex-

6*

ception, whereas we well know that our Lord only meant such rich men as were unduly attached to their riches. The same middle term "rich man" is used distributively in the minor premise, and the conclusion informs us that Crœsus will be lost simply because he is a rich man. The reverse of this is the fallacy of composition. Dr. Whately says there is no fallacy more common or more likely to deceive than the one now before us.

9. We often deduce false conclusions from principles that are correct when taken in their legitimate sense. Because we are commanded to restore to every man his own, we should not infer that we ought to restore his deadly weapons to a man transported with rage.

10. It is also false reasoning to conclude that a man has acted wrong because he did not succeed in an enterprise: or again, that his conduct is virtuous because he did succeed; for wise and good men often fail, and wicked enterprises sometimes succeed.

FOURTH PART.

Question. What is Method.

Answer. It is that part of logic which furnishes counsels and lays down rules for assisting us in the study of compound subjects; it helps us to discover hidden things, to dispel the obscurity which veils certain subjects, and to obtain a clearer understanding of the connections and relations that subsist among a variety of parts.

A general definition of method is, the art of arranging our ideas in such manner that we may discover truth when ignorant of it, or demonstrate it to others when we have found it.

Q. How many kinds of method are there?

A. Two: Analysis and Synthesis.

Q. Define the analytic method.

A. The analytic method is that by which we ascend from the conclusion to principles, or from effect to cause. It is generally used for discovering truth.

Q. Define the synthetic method.

A. The synthetic method is that by which we

descend from principles to consequences, or from cause to effect. It is used for demonstrating truth to others; it therefore supposes that the truth is already known.

Therefore there are two kinds of method, one *analysis*, by means of which we learn how to discover truth, the other synthesis, by means of which we communicate the truth acquired.

Analysis is not used for treating an entire science, but in resolving its questions. There are questions of words and questions of things.

I style questions of words (says Descartes), not those in which words are sought, but those in which by means of words we seek things, as in enigmas, or the explanation of what an author means by certain obscure or ambiguous words.

Questions of things, says again Descartes, may be reduced to four principal kinds.

1. When we seek causes by effects. Ex.; We know the various effects of the magnet, we seek the cause: we know that the tides ebb and flow, we inquire into the cause of these remarkable fluctuations, so powerful and so regular.

2. When we endeavor to trace effects from causes. Ex.; The ancients knew that wind and water had a superior power for moving bodies, but they never applied them, as do the moderns, to lessening the amount of manual labor, or to

other uses beneficial to mankind; which is the true aim of all Natural Philosophy. Observe that the first kind of question, seeking causes by ffects, belongs to the Theory of Natural Philosophy and the second, tracing effects from causes, constitutes the practice.

3. The third kind is, when from parts we try to discover a whole: as by adding several numbers we seek the amount; or by multiplying two numbers try to find the product.

4. The fourth is, when having a whole and one part, we seek the other part; or having a number and something to take from it we seek the difference.

But it is necessary to observe, that to extend these questions fully, so that they may comprise what can not properly be referred to the first two, we must take the word *part*, generally, for all that is included in an object, as its modes, extremities, accidents, properties, and all its attributes. Thus it would be seeking a whole by its parts, to find the area of a triangle by its given height and base; and on the contrary it would be seeking a part by the whole, and another part, to find the side of a rectangle by its given area and one of its sides.

In whatever manner the question is to be resolved or is stated, the first step, is to understand clearly *what is required*, in other words the exact point of the question.

For we should avoid what too often occurs with persons who hasten to solve a proposed question before maturely considering by what marks they may recognize the object of their search when they meet it. They resemble a servant, who, on being ordered by his master to seek a friend, hastens to be off, without informing himself who that friend is.

It is certain that in every question there is something unknown, otherwise there would be nothing to discover; however it is essential that that unknown object be characterized by certain conditions which determine us to look for one thing rather than another, and that may lead us to decide when we have attained the particular object of our inquiry.

We must first examine those conditions, observing not to add any thing which is not included in the proposed point, and not to omit any thing which it should comprise; for we may err in either way.

We should err in the former manner if, for example, being asked " *What animal walks on four feet in the morning; two at noon; and three in the evening;*" we imagined ourselves obliged to take the words *feet, morning, noon,* and *evening* in their literal sense; for the person who composed the enigma did not require this condition; therefore it is sufficient to take the words in their metaphorical sense, and the question would be correctly solved by answering *man*.

It is in the same manner that the pupil who has not learned the elements of Natural Philosophy, finds the marvelous in Tantalus's cup; or in the trick of the water drinker, who after taking a portion of water from his tankard, pours the remaining contents into several tumblers, each of which exhibits water of a brilliant, and different hue. The first problem is easily seen, consists in the vase containing water to a certain height, which it can not pass, and therefore must descend when it has attained the place determined, and the second consists in putting the colors wanted in the bottom of each tumbler.

Sometimes questions are proposed surrounded by a quantity of useless conditions, purposely intended to keep the mind of the examiner from perceiving the real point.

Another cause of failure in examination of the conditions sought, is the omission of conditions that are essential to the question proposed.

When the conditions that characterize the unknown in a question have been strictly examined then pass to the known; because it is by the known that we must discover the unknown. It is in this attention to defining clearly the known, that the art of analyzing chiefly consists; for it consists in deducing a number of truths which may lead us to decide upon the truth we seek. We will therefore give some general rules, by the help of which we may easily avoid the defects that are too often found in examination and demonstration.

GENERAL RULES COMMON TO ANALYSIS AND SYNTHESIS.

First Rule. Never employ terms that are obscure or equivocal in their meaning; or if they are employed, explain the sense in which they are to be taken. Disputes are frequently founded upon words alone, and this would not occur if care were taken to explain the meaning of the terms employed in the treatment of the question.

Second Rule. Never admit any but self-evident truths as axioms. An axiom has already been defined to be a truth which no one can dispute.

Third Rule. In questions purely philosophical consider as certain only what is evident, or evidently proved.

Fourth Rule. Endeavor to pass from the easy to the difficult, from the known to the unknown, arranging the propositions in a continuous chain of argument.

RULES PECULIAR TO ANALYSIS.

METHOD OF INVENTION.

First Rule. Examine the question thoroughly, and when you understand it well, express it with as much clearness and simplicity as possible.

Second Rule. If the proposed question comprises several particular questions, divide it into all its particular questions and resolve each of them.

The limits of the human intellect render it incapable of entertaining a number of subjects at the same time, therefore it becomes absolutely necessary to consider them separately.

Third Rule. Having compared the particular questions, endeavor to diminish their number, until you succeed in reducing them to one, which solution contains what we wish to know.

Fourth Rule. Look for intermediate ideas to aid in the resolution of particular questions. Begin by recalling to mind whatever previous knowledge you may have acquired on the proposed question, and by means of this former acquaintance with your subject, or by profoundly meditating on all the ideas which have any connection with it, you will easily obtain the answer required.

First Rule. Having determined the signification of such terms as may be obscure, next propose the axioms from which you intend deducing conclusions in proof of the truth that you wish to demonstrate. If you are going to employ a principle which is not a true axiom, and therefore needs proof, either prove this principle at once, or else give notice that you will do it in the course of your reasoning. If an appeal is to be made to an indisputable proposition, it should be placed directly after the axioms.

Second Rule. If your subject is compound, try to divide it so that its parts may be treated separately, and try also to treat the simpler parts before the more complex; but the divisions should, as much as possible, follow the order of nature.

Third Rule. Conclusions should be derived

from axioms, appeals, or propositions already proved, and that, by evident reasoning.

Fourth Rule. Let such propositions as are intended to demonstrate others precede these, and as far as possible, place the simple before the compound, those less compound before those more compound, always observing to studiously reject whatever is irrelevant to the proposed question.

OF THE METHOD OF STUDYING.

ARTICLE FIRST.

OF READING.

Question. What are the best means for rendering reading useful?

Answer. Frequently question yourself on the subject of your reading, and thus find out whether you have seized the precise meaning of the ideas presented. The rules in the chapter on Argumentation will be very proper for guides in this work of self-tuition. After reading a few volumes according to this method, you will be able to distinguish periods, subjects, and their proofs with great celerity. This method may be aptly compared to the progressive steps we made, when we learned the art of reading.

We began by distinguishing the shapes of the letters, then combined them into syllables and words, of which we formed phrases, and so on, until at last we read fluently without even thinking of the letter, syllable or word.

If we accustomed ourselves betimes to the prac· tice of carefully weighing the meaning of what we read, and reflecting upon it, we should attain facility in comprehending the ideas of others, we . should insensibly appropriate them, and while laying up a fund of thoughts for future use, avoid the too common occurrence of assigning to authors a meaning that they never intended to convey.

When we read, it should be with a view to profit, and therefore we should select a volume that will contribute to this end. A work that is worth reading should not be hastily conned over, skipping pages and even chapters, in order to dwell upon detached portions ; but it should be carefully and leisurely read, from the preface to the last sentence. We should consider the parts in the places that they hold in their own system, and in the light they throw upon one another. Whatever appears clear and sensible should be noted, so that if we meet any thing doubtful or equivocal it may serve for explanation or illustration.

If in any chapter the author's views seem to be less clearly exposed. the sense of phrases to be less accurately expressed, suspend your decisions until you have compared these parts with the context.

Compare the various parts of the work that you are reading with each other, and with other works on the same subject.

Beware of taking the figurative meaning for the literal meaning, and only dwell upon the beauties of style in order to glean practical principles.

Although the above rules are simple and easy to be followed, there are few young ladies who are willing to adopt them. There can be no doubt that unmethodical reading is the source of the very insignigcant profit they derive from the vast multitude of books which they devour. It would be well for them to reflect that by reading with care they will often fall upon phrases that contain maxims that are worth whole sections of propositions, and by studying words, they would correct a very general habit among young ladies, of misunderstanding the value of adjectives and interjections, and of applying them unnecessarily and inappropriately.

It is more important to read with care than with order. Do not read every book that is written on any subject that interests you, but consult an experienced and safe guide. Ill regulated reading produces confusion in the ideas, uncertainty, with tenacious adherence to pecu· liar views, and is too often the cause of that indistinctness and want of mental power that we observe in the conversations of young ladies. Always complete the perusal of one author, before you attempt another, at least on the same subject. The more you charge the memory the less it will retain, and besides the new subject will be likely to efface the impression that the other was beginning to form.

When circumstances beyond your control force you to commit to memory, or to read simultaneously more subjects than you have time to examine with care, exercise your memory in acquiring what is assigned you, and defer a more critical attention to your earliest leisure.

When you wish to acquire a science, always begin by studying its principles, and never leave a chapter without having rendered yourself familiar with its various propositions and divisions.

ARTICLE SECOND.

OF ABRIDGMENTS.

·It sometimes happens that we think we are in possession of a subject, when in reality our ideas are quite vague and indistinct. We are undeceived when, in attempting to commit our science to paper, we find ourselves in such complete embarrassment, that we are forced to review our text-book, digest the thoughts and elucidate their signification. Another signal advantage gained by writing the ideas of an author is, that these ideas become indentified with our own, and we also learn to invent new ones.

After these preliminary steps, you may carefully peruse a well-written paper on a chosen subject, then lay it aside and compose an essay on the same topic. Compare your work in its various features with the work selected, and profit by your failure or success. This is an excellent means of learning to write original compositions.

ARTICLE THIRD.

METHOD OF FORMING STYLE.

Style is the peculiar manner in which a writer expresses his thoughts. The mental characteristics of authors are revealed in their diction, a brilliant fancy produces a brilliant style, ardent passions and emotions a vehement manner of expression, a serious thoughtful inclination is apt to exhibit itself in a cold and formal mode of conveying thought.

But every writer should modify his natural manner, reduce it to conformity with the principles of good taste, and vary it according to subjects and circumstances.

You have learned in the elements of grammar that words are primitive or derivative, simple or compound. You have been exercised in combining words and phrases, and studying all that is necessary to render sentences grammatical.

The next step is to study precision, by rejecting all that is superfluous, avoiding frequent repetition of the same or similar words, and the incorrect use of synonymous words. Study we

the genius of the language in which you intend
to write, for every tongue has not only its idiom
but other characteristics, and these change too
with different epochs and with national character. "The vivacity of the Frenchman, the
gravity of the Spaniard, and the thoughtfulness
of the Englishman are unmistakably impressed
on their respective tongues." The style in one
language should be diffuse, in another concise;
one leaves much to be understood, another has
few ellipses; in some languages particles are
used for ornament, and in others they are rejected
when not necessary. Latin and English admit
of inversion, French shuns it. Compound words
contribute much to the strength of Greek,
French avoids them, but nearly all English words
of Saxon origin are consolidated compounds.
The English requires variety of expression, the
French allows none but what springs from
variety of thought. "Some languages excel in
particular modes of style, the English may be
used with respectable success in any style, as is
proved by its masterpieces in prose and poetry.*

Beauty of style depends upon a good selection
of words, and their accurate arrangement according to good sense and the genius of the lan-

* G. P. Quackenbos.

7

guage ; but it arises principally from thought.
We take pleasure in perusing an author who
thinks accurately and nobly, and expresses himself as he thinks. We like brevity when it does
not mislead us by rendering the subject obscure,
and when the succession of ideas is not so rapid
as to fatigue the attention. A writer expresses
himself with this agreeable conciseness or
brevity when he is master of his subject, is
well versed in the connection and depend-
ence of its parts, and is careful to throw such
lights as are necessary to leave no step in his
course unappreciated. Style thus characterized
will be vigorous and forcible if the subject de-
mand it, or delicate, if the writer restricts himself within proper limits, and allows things to be
readily perceived when grave motives hinder
him from expressing them.

An elevated style must proceed from the nature of the subject treated—and sublime writing can never be produced on any other than a
sublime theme. Good sense and delicacy of
taste must direct a writer in the use of embel-
lishments, the nature and use of which, with all
that appertains to the formation of style, are
given at length in a variety of popular works in
both French and English. Even Latin and
Greek grammars are now published by which

young ladies may acquire a knowledge of the structure and spirit of words and sentences in those model tongues, and which would aid them materially in studying the etymology of their own language.

Certain things require to be said with great simplicity; the mind is satisfied with a passing view of them; but there are others on which attention delights to repose: these should be presented several times, but when reproduced the expression should be changed, and the style employed be less diffuse, because a thought is more readily appreciated when it appears a second time.

As beauty of style must be felt by each reader, it is not astonishing that the epithets beautiful, elegant, &c. are not always well applied. If affectation prompts a writer to leave the beaten path and strike out into novel expressions, his style, far from exciting admiration, will be simply denominated ridiculous; but if, without desiring to attract notice, he devotes himself to thinking accurately, penetrating to the bottom of his subject, unveiling its secret springs and delicate relations, and then expresses himself conformably to his ideas, it is certain that he will excel in composition, because he excels in thought.

When we read or study an author who impresses us with an exalted idea of his capacity, we should examine his manner of clothing his ideas, and endeavor to discover by what means he was able to produce so desirable an effect.

We should also inquire into the causes of any displeasure provoked by the perusal of an author; the inquiries satisfied may prove of great utility in the formation of a good style; for we can thus avoid the defects which have displeased us, and use the method which a successful author adopted to command admiration.

THE END.

* 9 7 8 3 7 4 1 1 8 5 3 2 8 *